THE LIFE OF H. R. H.
The Duke of Flamborough

H.R.H. PRINCE AUGUSTUS
THIRD DUKE OF FLAMBOROUGH

The Life of
H. R. H.
The Duke of Flamborough

BY

Benjamin Bunny

A FOOTNOTE TO HISTORY,
ARRANGED EXPURGATED, AND EDITED

BY

LAURENCE HOUSMAN

New York
PAYSON AND CLARKE LTD
1929

CONTENTS

Illustrations

EDITOR'S INTRODUCTION

ABOUT five years ago I was placed in a position of considerable difficulty by the delivery into my hands (for consideration first, and for a consideration afterwards) of a manuscript which presented me with a moral problem.

Is one justified in destroying a work of literary beauty on account of its intimacy or of its pernicious morals? Lady Burton (of Victorian character in more ways than one) answered that question in the affirmative; and a Persian Garden was burned to ashes in consequence.

But though I am Victorian, I am not Lady Burton; and I am sure that anything which I found beautiful I should save from the flames, however naughtily expressed – since, in my view of the world, beauty came long before morals, does so still, is the more important product, and is the more likely to survive.

But in this case it was not beauty I had to consider, but history and human document, inextricably mixed up with what was mani-

9

festly fiction. If the thing had any historical foundation, or even conveyed a true lesson in human nature, was I to reject and delete it from the land of the living, because the writer of it had indulged in a romantic fancy far exceeding the residuum of fact on which it was based? Or was it possible, as an alternative, to pick out the facts and cast the fancies away?

I saw, at a glance, that it was not; for even the things which might be true were so fancifully told that separation seemed impossible. If it was at all history, it belonged to the new school just then beginning to make its mark – the school which recognizes that history itself is a great work of fiction, contemporarily provided for the generations that follow, by that mingled gang of liars and half-truth-tellers who control the destinies and diplomacy of nations, and for the justification of their wars can – when it suits their purpose – forge or suppress documents, alter dates, or lay up in store, as proof of their pacific policies, despatches which were never despatched, nor ever intended to be despatched to their addressees.

And how is the future historian to know, with such a shoal of red-herrings criss-crossing his path, which way in that bygone age truth really went? The thing we see most plainly, which – through all murder – will out, is that mysterious thing called character. And so it is upon character that history fixes rightly and most resolutely to-day.

It was when history was beginning to be so written, that a directed chance put into my hands this document, so indistinguishably compounded of possible fact and impossible fiction; which, after startled reading, and the subsequent transaction which made it mine, I was reluctant to destroy – not only because I had paid good money for it, but because it might have in it more microbes of truth than at first seemed at all probable.

But I saw clearly that, if truth were in it, it was of so scaring a kind, and so lacking in corroborative evidence, that I could not make myself responsible for its appearance without a full statement of its very doubtful credentials, and a certain tactful adaptation of the text in matters personal, of which the intelligent reader may possibly become aware.

And so, having thus prepared the way with due caution, I ask readers not to regard as other than fiction anything which they here find difficult to believe, or, if believable, too scandalous in its implications to please comfortable minds. I am quite sure that the writer was a romantic; and romantics are generally victims of a quality in themselves, which leaves them incapable of distinguishing fancy from fact. I have more than a suspicion that, even when he is telling of something that really did happen, the writer is not necessarily telling it of the right person.

How I came by the substance of what follows, the reader may thus picture to himself: On a very wet day a postman's knock; a wet parcel of dirty manuscript dirtily addressed; with it a letter stating that the sender would, on hearing from me, do himself the honour to call and make terms for the surrender of all rights – even to the claim of authorship – in what he regarded as 'an historical document of no little importance.' He was mine obediently; Richard Bunny his name. The manuscript, I saw, purported to be by Benjamin Bunny; Richard Bunny was his son.

A few days later an incredibly shabby individual presented himself. I had not written asking him to come, for I was still in doubt. He was anxious to know, he said, whether the manuscript had reached me.

He was also quite frank in his inquiries into my character. Was I, he asked, an author capable of publishing as my own something which was not really mine? I told him that I had once done so inadvertently. I did not tell him the story, I have done so elsewhere, and I hope that Mr. Yone Noguchi has forgiven me.

He seemed pleased with my admission. 'Then it will be well worth your while,' he said, 'to buy this and pretend you wrote it.'

'It may be more worth my while,' I replied, 'to pretend that I didn't write it. I did that once with another book, and made a considerable success of it.'

'That's as you like,' he replied; 'I'm not particular so long as I get my price.'

I asked him why, if he thought it good, he had not offered it to a publisher? He replied – what I believe is generally true – that publishers nowadays refuse to look at manuscripts that are not typewritten; five had sent it back to him unread. It would cost about seven pounds to type, and he hadn't the money.

I then asked him his price.

In the course of the next five minutes his price varied considerably. His real price was that he wanted to get to America; and to get there quick before his present passport expired. He had reason to doubt, apparently, whether he could ever get it renewed.

To inspire me with more sympathy if not

confidence, he told me a little of his life. He had been a valet, like his father before him, and named a few of the places and families where he had seen service.

Having sampled the manuscript, I was more interested in his father. What about him? I asked. He had, as I surmised, been dead for a good many years. Richard, the son, was himself rather more than elderly. Benjamin, I then heard, had been born under peculiar circumstances – circumstances which are touched on in the following narrative; his mother a serving-maid, his father a footman, he had come to them in wedlock, too soon for respectability, too soon also, as in late life he had discovered, to have any valid claim to that on which for fifty years he had pinned his faith.

And finding then that he had given a life of faithful service to one whom he had believed to be his father, but who was in fact no relation to him whatever, he compensated himself for his disappointment by writing the 'Life' embodied in the manuscript which was now offered me.

The material? There was no concealment about that; his employment had given him opportunities which he had sedulously used during a service of thirty years; in seeking to

establish proof of a biological connection
between himself and that other, he had
acquired materials for a biography.

So much, then, was explained. But the
manuscript, which I had already looked into,
did not strike me as having so casual an origin
– the product of an afterthought in the brain
of a valet suffering from disappointed parent-
worship. He was obviously a well-educated
man – his pen the pen of a ready writer.

In answer to my interrogations upon this
point, the son explained that, for a good many
years, his father had contributed paragraphs
and short articles to society journals during the
'seventies and the 'eighties, from the information about personages in high life which came
to him so easily behind the scenes; that he got
a good price for them, and on one occasion
was able to back his paragraph – a paragraph
of exceedingly good 'copy' – with such precise
and well-informed details as to save the journal
which published it from a threatened libel
action. He might even, shortly after, have
become sub-editor, his means for obtaining
society gossip having proved so extensive and
so reliable; but still obsessed with that mistaken
idea as to his origin, he let the opportunity go;
and a few years later, having been caught

making secret investigations into the private papers of his employer, within a few days of his death, was dismissed without a character, and after writing the 'Life,' for which no publisher could be found, had died, leaving the manuscript to his son, who also had had no luck with it: from whom, indeed, at some date or other, and for reasons into which I did not inquire, luck seemed bodily to have parted.

So here I had before me the case of a book born out of time, useless to the man who had written it, and of no more use that he could discover to the man who had inherited it – a book written in the nineteenth century which could only be published in the twentieth.

Twentieth-century publishers had refused to look at it because it was in dirty and rather illegible manuscript. I looked at it because what is dirty and illegible has a stealthy attraction for me; I have a fancy that some day, by following out this instinct, I may light at last on the autograph writing of the real Shakespeare.

This manuscript, what with waiting and with many fruitless goings to and fro, had become so soiled and torn, that life of any kind would not much longer be in it; I felt that, if I did nothing to rescue it, it was likely to disappear.

I offered, therefore, the best advice in my
power: I told this 'Visiter' (though indeed no
longer young) that he would have done much
better to go to Sir James Barrie, or blow his
wreathèd Horn at the gates of Mr. John Gals-
worthy, leaving his father's photograph in the
letter-box for proof of authenticity; I said that
Mr. Shaw, or Mr. Strachey could give him a
far better advertisement. But he only replied
with meek persistence: 'I have come to you,
sir, I thought *you* would be interested.'

And the testimonial thus accorded me by that
down-and-out specimen of failed humanity
pleased me better than the praise of many critics;
for humanity with its curiosities, rather than
literature, is my line. And so we negotiated a
price, which did not go lower than that which
he had last named. America, as a land of
liberty, was the mirage toward which his glaz-
ing eyes were turned.

He is safe now oversea, if anyone can be
called 'safe' in America: safe from the hands
of *our* police at any rate. And if this 'Life'
attracts any attention at all, readers may be
glad to know that the derelict son of Mr.
Benjamin Bunny will share the benefit.

THE LIFE OF H. R. H.
The Duke of Flamborough

CHAPTER I

BIRTH, PARENTAGE, AND CHILDHOOD

AUGUSTUS WILLIAM CARL JOSEPH EMMANUEL, the only son of his princely parents the Duke and Duchess of Flamborough, was born at the castle of Steinburg on the Rhine, on a 25th day of March early in the nineteenth century; and, for the first two months of his existence, was, in a prospective sense, the most important person in the world then living.

For those two months he had – or his parents had for him – the very highest expectations, though mingled with a dash of doubt. The succession to the throne of his fathers, but not of his race, was just then in an exiguous and withering condition. Like a ripe heifer turned loose into a field of oxen, the royal inheritance had unseasonably' hung fire for a number of years; during that time hope of posterity had either been lacking or had died young.

The oxen – brothers and uncles – had been capable of much in the past, but now apparently were not to be relied on, though German brides of a child-bearing type had been found for them; and though as a final duty to king and country six out of eight had settled down to the dull doom of matrimony, only two of these gave any sign of useful and practical results.

Of these the first and the most forward, by the grace of his good wife Princess Wilhelmina Caroline of Thurm-Turingen, was H.R.H. second Duke of Flamborough, and, in the line of succession to the throne of his Father (now so near his demise), fourth among eight brothers, all, in the reputable sense, childless – without heirs, that is to say.

A little behind in acceptance of matrimony had come number three, the Duke of Bendigo; but he dying soon after, and his wife not in her first youth by any means, there had remained a doubt. This doubt, however, was now resolving itself – hopefully for the House of Bendigo, less hopefully for the House of Flamborough, which in its own interests wished things, very naturally, to be otherwise.

Nevertheless, in an almost neck and neck race of wife versus widow, wife won; and for two months, H.R.H. Augustus William Carl Joseph Emmanuel lived, moved, and had his being as a prospective monarch whose rights, temporarily at any rate, there was none to dispute.

That being so, his birth had of necessity to be very circumspectly attended; for just as, here in England, we still search the cellars of our House of Commons for a possible Guy Fawkes at each opening of Parliament, so, when an heir is born to any European throne, a similar search or watch is instituted against any possible repetition of the 'Warming-pan Plot,' which having been invented in one country may actually happen in another.

And so, some days or weeks before his expected arrival, there came very importantly from oversea, with signed and sealed credentials, plenipotentiaries and experts – not in the art of midwifery, but in the law and constitutional practice of monarchical primogeniture – to attend, watch, certify, and register the event with such thoroughness that no question of it could ever thereafter arise. Though fools might rush in unavoidably in the course of nature, warming-pans must be constitutionally kept out, or at least carefully examined as to their contents before introduction for bed-warming purposes could be allowed.

The plenipotentiaries were – that one of the Royal Dukes whose interest in the succession came next; Lord Sago, Ambassador to the Rhineland, specially appointed for the time, and the Right Hon. John Montague Rice, Writer to the Signet and Privy Councillor. By these, with signatures appended, the following safeguarding document was issued upon the day of birth:

'We the undersigned, [names and dignities here follow] specially instructed to attend the Confinement of H.R.H. the Duchess of Flamborough, do hereby solemnly declare that, having been apprised by H.R.H. the Duke of Flamborough, at a quarter before one of the clock on the morning of March 25th in the year of our Lord 18—, that Her Royal Highness's labour pains had commenced, we did straightway together, each in the other's presence, and of intent purpose, all being in our right minds, repair forthwith to the room adjoining that in which Her Royal Highness was to be delivered, the door between these two rooms remaining open during the whole of our attendance; and that having been previously informed by His Royal Highness that Her Royal Highness would be confined in HER

H.R.H. ERNEST GEORGE
SECOND DUKE OF FLAMBOROUGH
Father of Prince Augustus

Bedroom up one pair of stairs, and that free access must remain from that room to HER Dressing-room immediately contiguous thereto, and these rooms having been previously shown to one of us – the Right Hon. John Montague Rice, the seal of the said John Montague Rice was affixed (so as to close it) to the outside and keyhole of the outward door of the said Dressing-room, under the directions of H.R.H. the Duke of Flamborough – He having locked the said door, and given the said key thereof to the said Right Hon. John Montague Rice, so that no communication with the Bedroom could thereafter take place from without but under our eyes, we remaining in the room adjoining the Bedroom, through which all persons entering the Bedroom must pass; that on arrival we found Her Royal Highness in the genuine experience of HER labour pains, and that sharp labour pains continued till ten minutes past two o'clock of the morning aforesaid, when Her Royal Highness was safely delivered of a male Child, whose sex we determined by actual inspection; and that said Child was alive and of sound health and limb at the said hour, and so continues to be at the time when, together, and each in the other's presence, we make this declaration affirming it to be true, and hereto affix our signatures in proof and witness thereof.'

Thus, signed, sealed, and safely delivered, with so much pomp and circumstance – heir presumptive to the crown of his adopted land – it is hardly to be wondered that in his early years Prince Augustus regarded the event which followed two months later as a gross mis-appropriation of rights which should have remained his own. In all other cases of which he knew, where royal inheritance operated, the male had definite precedence of the female, sometimes even to the total exclusion of her claim in any circumstance whatsoever; and since for two months he had been the recognized heir, it was difficult to persuade him that any law of succession, rightly interpreted, could have deprived him of what was once his, in favour of the partially disqualified sex. It may be doubted, indeed, whether, even in his maturer years, he ever came to understand so shifty a proviso as that which put into the mouth of his cousin, Princess Augusta, the plum which had once been in his own.

Even in the matter of names she elbowed and got the better of him, making his to appear foolish. His had come first; but the Duchess of

26

Bendigo, in anticipation of her own event, had, it appears, made an unalterable choice, and though defeated of a son, would not be defeated of a name. Augustus was good; but Augusta sounded comparatively better.

The two Duchesses exchanged compliments, but family affection in such a case was hardly to be looked for; there was no intercourse, no intimacy; nor did the rival hopes meet for a good many years. Care had been taken that Augusta should be born in the capital of the country over which she was to rule, and in that country she spent her entire youth and got all her education. But Augustus, having been born abroad in a part of the world where his father had fewer debts than at home, and where the upkeep of royal state was less expensive, remained abroad for the first fourteen years of his life, at the Court of his uncle the Reigning Duke of Thurm-Turingen, where a sound German education was poured over him, but luckily did not penetrate sufficiently to do harm; only in the matter of pronunciation did it remain ineradicable, but in the royal circle hardly noticeable, since there it was only a matter of degree, and though a diminishing one, had become almost a tradition.

Of this period of his life only one or two

events stand out worth recording, as having left some mark upon his character or affected his future career. A family nurse, named Mrs. Quickly, gave him an early smattering of the tongue which his future position would oblige him to use on public occasions. A little later he learned French; but German remained his mother tongue, the only one in which he was able to think with ease, or spell fairly correctly.

At the age of five he very nearly succumbed to an attack of scarlet fever. Under the accepted medical treatment of the day he was gradually sinking, and the hopes of the House of Flamborough with him, when his life was saved by a big dose of Rhenish wine administered by his distracted father. Made mildly drunk by the potion, he fell asleep, threw off his delirium, reduced his temperature, and recovered.

This illness affected his hair. During youth it remained plentiful, but had little staying power left in it; in his early twenties he began to go bald, and, though often advised to do so for appearance' sake, refused resolutely to wear a wig. A head like a bullet was not, he conceived, unbecoming to the Commander-in-Chief of an army.

This sort of common sense, touched by sym-bolism, remained a characteristic through life. In the written directions for the coffining of his royal remains, many years later, were these words: 'Bury my walking-stick with me, the one with the bone handle mounted in gold; it has been a good friend, never letting me down.' Sword, cocked hat, and spurs were to be left outside, for these had let him down sadly at the last. Yet his heart was with the army, and for that reason, when he died, was broken.

His nurse was more fortunately chosen than his first tutor, from whom he had a more narrow escape than from the scarlet fever. A fever of another kind, but of the same colour, took hold of this unfortunate man, proving his unsuitability for the slow task which had been imposed on him. Either he lacked patience and perseverance, or had not the gift for communicating that minimum of knowledge which was expected of him. And so, having tried in vain for some months to instil an understanding of constitutional government into the slow un-plodding brain of his pupil, he conceived himself summoned of the Lord to offer him up a sacrifice for the well-being of the people he might otherwise be called on to rule. One night strange sounds being heard in the Prince's chamber, the tutor was found on his knees by the bed (in which Prince Augustus lay gagged and bound) uttering a dedicatory prayer for the salvation of the monarchical system, and with sacrificial knife already uplifted for the blow.

The Prince's life was saved, but the shock to his system was great; and ever afterwards, whenever he found himself suddenly prevented from anything he had planned or greatly set his heart on, all the symptoms of a healthy resistance to gagging and binding became manifest, and he would make a great noise, using violent gestures as well as language.

An instance of this occurred in quite early days, when on being prevented by his nurse from going into a field of cows to pick buttercups, he fell into such excited antics and uncouth gestures that he frightened away not only his nurse but the cows. And when the nurse, reporting epilepsy, returned with medical aid, she found Prince Augustus restored to his right mind with a large bunch of buttercups for proof.

But the remarkable thing about that earlier escape from a violent death is that he had no memory of the incident, and when, many years later, he came upon family letters giving an account of it. he made a marginal note that the whole thing was a cock-and-bull story and that to his knowledge nothing of the kind had ever occurred.

In the present psychological age this has become more explainable; but there is no doubt whatever that the shock did permanently impair his understanding of things in general, and of constitutional monarchy in particular. And while it made him outwardly submissive, and on the whole obedient, to the subsequent tutors from whom he received instruction, it left him with a curious inability to be himself while in their company. And so, though in the main a simple character, he became two people; the one timid, lacking in self-confidence and initiative, and with an artificially exaggerated conscience; the other crude, bullying, impulsive, at times irresponsible, doing incalculable things in a blind headstrong way, of which he only became properly conscious when the whole affair was over.

The child is indeed father of the man; but the child also has fathers other than its own parent. And it is quite possible that the character of Prince Augustus was, in certain of its aspects, more deeply stamped and fathered by that incident which thereafter remained forgotten, than by the slow daily training which, from then on, befell his youth. One would not, indeed, think from the record of that period left to us in his own handwriting that his nature had in it any fire at all. We might even follow up that record day by day to his seventeenth year before discovering our mistake.

But if the reader will be patient through two more chapters the discovery will be made.

CHAPTER II

DUTY, AND A DIARY

PRINCE AUGUSTUS began to keep a diary in his seventh year; and by it we learn better than by any other record what kind of training his mind underwent from then on till his youth had fulfilled itself.

It was obviously a diary written to order, and open daily to the inspection of those who had charge of him, forming indeed the very centre of the educational system to which his character was subjected – a kind of Protestant confessional compulsorily imposed for the good of his soul. In it we trace the gradual development of an arrested growth, his reactions to discipline, instruction, authority, society, and religion. A free growth it could not be called, but the growth was there in a sideway direction; and daily his tutors tended it, correcting with painstaking thoroughness the spelling, the grammar, and the sentiments.

C

These diaries still exist – an almost unbroken array extending from childhood to adolescence; then, with a few breaks, carried on to within a few months of his death. In them we have the written and regimented conscience of a rather ordinary mind, containing, therefore, nothing very impressive or original; but where, on rare occasions – mainly in early adolescence – the ordinary mind breaks loose and asserts itself free of supervision, they are illuminating.

His first diary was encouragingly given to him, as a present on his seventh birthday; and thus deceptively blinkered, he begins cheerfully acknowledging the gift from his 'dear Mamma'; and with the hope that it will teach him to write and spell more correctly, sets forth all unawares to deliver himself up into a bondage which is to last for years.

In the first week, as the self-examining conscience gets into its well-disciplined stride, we read thus:

'My tutor tells me that my spelling is very bad. It is very important that I should correct this, and I will do it as well as I know how. I had a bath last night. Pie-bald horses are so because of their ancestry. This is very curious, but cannot I suppose be otherwise. But why are not men sometimes pie-bald too, since there are both black as well as white?'

A few months later we read:

'I am studying geography, I find Europe is much smaller than I supposed. It is a remarkable dispensation of God that so small a portion of the world should be in advance of the much larger and older countries as regards civilization and morals. That is also why it is right that we should go and conquer them. I ought to be very grateful that my own country though it is so small in appearance has been called to rule over so large a number of the less fortunate nations, and will probably some day have more. As I am going into the army I must give this my attention and see God's hand in it.'

.   .   .   .   .

'My dear parents have given me a pony as a new year's gift; so I must now learn to ride it. It is to be hoped that I do not fall off so often as to discourage me. But that, my tutor tells me, is one of my great faults which I must correct.'

The next day comes the following entry:

'I did not do my first ride well, but I pray that with perseverance I may improve. When

35

I am older my legs will be longer and will help me to ride better. I do not see till that happens how I can do as well as I am expected to do; but my tutor says that I must, and I know that he is always right.

'I went to-day to see my two Cousins Amelia and Charlotte of Thurm-Turingen confirmed. It was a very solemn sight. The Bishop did it; and there were a great many people looking on. The chapel was very crowded because it was so small, and I felt very hot and uncomfortable though I had one of the best places.'

.   .   .   .   .

'The King and Queen of Hanover are here on a visit. This is the first time that I have seen a crowned head; but being with relatives they did not wear them which I had hoped they would do. All the Hanoverians, it seems, are great eaters of supper, which has become a sort of national costume,[1] and of which they are proud. I am told that the King and Queen are both large eaters and very fast at it, so it makes them more popular when they have the people of Hanover to dine with them. I must remember this as it may be useful to know oneself.'

.   .   .   .   .

'My tutor tells me that I ought not to write in

[1] This the tutor has corrected to 'custom.' .

36

my diary things which people tell me which
are not true or important. It is very important
that I should train myself to be respectful even
in my secret thoughts toward my betters, and
especially toward Kings and Queens as without
them the world could not go on. It is a very
solemn thought that one day I might have to
be a King myself; but if my dear Cousin
Augusta continues to be spared to us that will
not happen, so I had better not think about it.'

.   .   .   .   .

'Again to-day I behaved rather cowardly
during my ride. This ought not to happen
again. It is a very besetting fault that I fall off
so often. During the last year I have grown an
inch and a half; but I fear I am still very back-
ward for my age both in my studies and in all
my ideas and behaviour generally. This I must
set myself to improve.'

.   .   .   .   .

'A fortnight ago I wrote to my Cousin
Augusta upon her birthday as my dear Mamma
said it was the correct thing to do ; and to-day
in consequence I received a very nice letter
from her in return. I notice that she writes and
spells much better than I do. This is very
humiliating, and I must correct it. I wonder
what my Cousin Augusta is like, and whether

37

she is in good health and as likely to live as I am. This I must hope and pray as I am told that her life is going to be a very decisive one to the nation. I wonder who is going to marry her. I hope I shall be married first.'

.   .   .   .   .

'My tutor says I am not to fill up my diary by copying things out of books, but only my own ideas and expressions. I have done this and now see that it was wrong. For how can I learn to express myself without practice. I must also think – which is often a great trial, but for one in my position is very necessary, since I must make a good appearance and be entitled to everyone's respect, for if my Cousin Augusta were to die I should have a great responsibility and a much greater position about which I try not to think.'

Thus we watch the slow tentative development; cautiously feeling his way to the good graces of his tutor, he passes from childhood to youth. His expressions and ideas do not greatly change; but we become aware of larger contacts with life and society. Publicity begins to claim him; he meets important people, goes to other places, attends royal receptions, sometimes is himself the show; and meanwhile the

commentary of his tutored conscience continues to toe the line laid down for it. This is
what he writes at the age of ten:

'My tutor tells me that I am falling into a
fresh fault, that of chattering too much when I
meet people. This I must correct; but it is
very difficult to know that one has a fresh fault
till one has fallen into it.'

Apparently new faults continue to declare
themselves; for a month later he writes:

'I have not remembered so many bad days
following so soon after each other for some
time. This is in a great degree owing to a bad
Sunday, which I did not spend in the proper
observance; and if one begins the week badly
on the day specially set apart for the practice
of good behaviour, the rest is sure to go wrong.
This being God's holy law and audience,[1] I
must see to it that I observe it myself before
I say anything about others.'

.   .   .   .   .

'Yesterday I was again violent and hasty, and
indeed might almost say that I did everything
wrong except remembering my prayers which

[1] This word the tutor has omitted to correct.

I now generally do, thanks to my tutor's constant reminders about it.'

.   .   .   .

'Another month has gone by. Have I been diligent in it, or behaved in it as I ought? I fear that too often I have not. Chattering is one of my chief faults and has begun to grow on me. Added to which, from being with others older than myself and who ought to know better, I have developed a tendency to swear, which I am told is not right; but if one is going into the army what else is one to do? I do not think that many battles have been won without a great deal of swearing; and I read the other day that there were some troops in Flanders which were famous for it. But perhaps I am too young as yet to judge of these things; and so for the present to participate in them is the sort of thing I must avoid.'

.   .   .   .   .

'My tutor has very kindly pointed out to me that it is unbecoming for me to use my diary as a vehicle for arguing against what he has told me is right. Indeed my most glaring fault now is that I desire to argue with everybody I meet and prove to them that they are wrong. I must however make up my mind to correct this, as otherwise it will bring me into the deserved contempt of my intellectual superiors, and only make me an object of dislike to my inferiors.'

    .   .   .   .

'Yesterday I again fell into that bad habit of mine to form hasty and prejudiced opinions, and speak hastily rather than thinking them over in my mind, and then saying my idea quietly when I have decided on it. I am then generally obliged to retract them which will become a very unfortunate thing hereafter when I have said them in public. I must really take great pains to avoid this. It is very discouraging as one grows older how much more difficult life becomes. What it will be like when I am grown up and before the public eye with so many responsibilities, *God only knows.*'

    .   .   .   .

'My tutor tells me that I ought not to lightly invoke the name of my Maker except in church; but he bids me let the expression stand now without correction but underlined as a warning for the future.'

    .   .   .   .

'I begin very much to fear that I shall never learn all the things that I ought to learn; life is so short and complicated. But as the wise Latin proverb remarks, "Nemo me lacessit

41

impune," "You cannot learn what is necessary without trouble"; so I will try and do likewise.'

Even these few extracts – the most varied and eventful that can be found in entries made daily, and extending over a period of nearly seven years – will have struck the reader by their monotony of thought and expression. What, then, must life itself have been like of which these are the bright particular flowers; or is it to be wondered that when an opportunity of change and release presented itself something approaching an outbreak should have occurred?

By the time Prince Augustus had reached the age of fourteen two deaths in the royal succession had taken place; and having been thus brought a couple of lives nearer to the throne, it was decided that he should no longer remain abroad, but go, for the completion of his education, to the court of the King his uncle, and there in the country to which in future he must belong, acquire the language, tastes, habits, and accomplishments required of one in the exalted position which would in any case be his, with a yet greater possibility lying behind it.

DUTY, AND A DIARY

With this change of environment it may be reckoned that the Prince's childhood ended; and his training from youth into manhood was begun.

CHAPTER III

GROWING PAINS

VERY graciously the old King receives him; they meet for the first time; and the Queen Consort proves herself a kind aunt. But though there is a change of scene with larger surroundings of pomp and circumstance, there is little or no change in the routine of his education.

It is true he acquires a new tutor who also becomes his chaplain – a foretaste of the dignity which will be his with a household of his own. But the system is the same. Word of the diary has been passed on; it lies open to daily inspection, and Prince Augustus writes in it accordingly.

The new inquisitor is the Hon. and Rev. Adolphus Tollet, who speedily finds fresh faults for him to fall into, not discovered by his predecessor. There is now the added difficulty of the new language with its illogical vagaries of spelling, in regard to which the possession of a mind equally illogical affords, alas, no help. And so we come soon on the following entry:

'It is really a most dreadful thing at my age that I am not perfect in spelling, particularly over proper names, which is going to be very important for me as I shall have to know so many. Mr. Tollet has in consequence desired me to learn a certain number of names every day for ten minutes after luncheon, which though a good thing is very degrading to a boy of nearly fourteen.

'Yesterday there was a dispute at luncheon between Lady Sophia, one of the ladies in attendance, and my dear Aunt the Queen, I being the innocent cause of it, having re-marked on Lady Sophia's good appetite, which indeed, when certain dishes she likes appear on the table, is very noticeable. I shall never now make any remarks in the King's or Queen's presence.'

.   .   .   .   .

'There is great trouble going on. The King being in need of more money has told the Queen she must reduce her expenses – by which he means give less in charities. It appears to be the rule that the Queen must only

45

give half what the King does for anything where the donations are made public. And the Queen has sometimes forgotten this or not agreed to it, being very generous to the poor and benevolent, as I am sure everybody is aware. And the Queen says that charity comes before luxuries, so has reduced the number of her horses which are more than she herself can make use of; and in consequence her Master of the Horse has resigned, which, I suppose, is because he has always been able to use them himself or make money by hiring them. And the King is very much annoyed. I am sure I don't know which I ought to think is in the right; and this is very painful for me.'

As a footnote the following is appended:

'Mr. Tollet tells me that I ought not to have written any of this down in my diary; but he once told me that I ought to take note of historical events; and I thought this might be one of them, as I am sure it has never happened before, and I don't think it ever will again, as the Queen's Master of the Horse has now come back, and there are as many horses in the stable as ever.'

.   .   .   .   .

'To-day is the last of the year. Alas, how

46

rapidly time flies, and what a serious thought
it is that that which has once gone by can never
be recalled. Have I spent the last year as I
ought? Next year brings great changes, I am
going to be confirmed and must then consider
myself more of a man. Truly we are living in
very extraordinary times.'

.   .   .   .   .

'Mr. Tollet has been looking through my
diaries. He says they are very childish and bad;
and yet all I have written there was to please
him. There is no greater duty involved on a
child than to obey their parents and not even
think that he knows better than they are. Mr.
Tollet explained to me yesterday that why so
many children now make this mistake is that
they are receiving a better education, and in consequence think that they may with impunity
follow their own ideas rather than theirs.'

.   .   .   .   .

'Chattering is still a great defect. I hope soon
to conquer my old faults of not liking to jump
and showing cowardice on a horse. There is
now the standing too near the fire which
Mamma speaks to me about. It seems to me
that I like to do nearly all the things which I
ought not to do. Life is a great mystery; but
how can one expect it to be otherwise, being

47

only human ourselves, and God so much our superior in every way that we can think of.'

.   .   .   .   .

'This year, since coming into a country where it will be expected of me, I have learned to swim; but I still find diving very difficult. It is so hard to think with one's head downward that one is going to be safe when one gets there. Yet to do otherwise is dangerous, for if one lets oneself in flat I find from experience that the shock is terrible and may even take the skin off. Shooting is also a thing I shall have to learn; but if one does not take a very determined hold and master the weapon thoroughly as one fires, it kicks terribly. It seems a lot of pain and trouble to go through for hitting a small bird which you are probably going to miss. Shooting elephants and big game would be different and ever so much easier and more worth while; and of course in the army the same sort of thing may have to be done. But I suppose I shall always be attached to the cavalry, where my chief difficulty will be the horses.'

.   .   .   .   .

'To-day is the King's sham birthday; but of course in the family we do not observe it, as we did that a month ago. Only outside we see the flags flying and hear the guns. It is a very useful way of reminding the nation that it has got to be loyal in order to be prosperous and contented; but otherwise is rather confusing. I do not know that I ever really want to be King; there are many things against it; but I think that to be a reigning Queen must be a greater misfortune for a woman; and this makes me feel very sorry for my Cousin Augusta if it should ever happen. But in any case I pray always that the King's present life may be spared; so there is no reason at present to think about it.'

.   .   .   .   .

'I understand from Mr. Tollet that it is the Queen's intention to examine me in the authorized articles of the Christian faith as established in this country, where it is slightly different from the one in which I was brought up.

'It is very difficult to remember what the changes are, or why. I am afraid I do not know all of them, and it is sad if in consequence I sometimes fall into heresy. This I must correct, as for one in my position orthodoxy is very important. It helps me to feel safe that I am forbidden by law ever to come to the throne if I become a Roman Catholic; so I do not have to think about that religion at all, or try to

49   D

understand it, as I have to do about my own.
But I cannot help wondering what would
happen if that were to happen to my Cousin
Augusta. I wonder if they have thought about
trying if it would not be a good thing.'

.   .   .   .

'Mr. Tollet tells me that the above are very
unbecoming expressions to have used, or indeed
the very idea of them. This is a sad thought
which I must endeavour to correct.'

It is evident from these and other extracts
that the question of the succession and his own
relation thereto was beginning to arouse his
active interest. Ancestry appealed to him; he
had it deeply in his blood.

Through this growing interest in his for-
bears, his tutor appears to have conceived the
idea of teaching him the rudiments of mathematics, other methods having failed; and for a
holiday task set him to count up the number
and names of his ancestors, on the female side
as well as the male.

This gave him a larger view of things than he
had yet conceived of. He discovered the fact
that he had four grandparents, eight great-
grandparents, sixteen twice great, thirty-two
thrice great, and so on in progression. By the

H.R.H. WILHELMINA CAROLINE
DUCHESS OF FLAMBOROUGH
Mother of Prince Augustus

time he got back to the sixth generation he had
traced his descent to all the royal and princely
houses of Europe; and though in the course
of his investigations he had discovered many
unhappy, broken, and diseased alliances, not
one had been a 'misalliance' in the conven-
tional sense of that word. The God of Kingship
and Royalty had presided triumphantly over
all of them.

This made him very satisfied and proud with
himself. It is true that in his research through
the ancestral archives he discovered that a
certain princely house from which he section-
ally derived had tails, and that in himself was
a rudiment of the same thing – a bony projec-
tion as though the base of the spine had taken
an unruly course of its own, different from other
spines. Hitherto this, having practical draw-
backs, had somewhat troubled and annoyed
him. Now he submitted to it as a proof that
his family tree in that direction was well and
truly founded; he hung on it by his tail, so to
speak.

Had he gone back a little further, or been
admitted to the more secret archives of that
branch of his origin, he would have discovered
that the tail had not in the first place been
come by reputably or legitimately; but had

been traced on its first appearance, with fright-
ful hullabalooings followed by hushings up, to
an interloper of more primitive race-char-
acteristics and of wholly inadequate rank – one
serving in the retinue of an ambassador to the
Grand Ducal Court at which presently the
birth took place. And had not the Grand Duke
died in the nick of time, urgently needing an
heir, there is little doubt that this particular
scion of the reigning line would have disappeared before the succession called for him.
As it was, however, the tail – after a long
minority – came into the title and remained
there, averaging for the first four generations
a two-inch excrescence – thereafter diminishing, and, in the Duke's case, almost negligible,
but accountable perhaps, since nothing else
could, for the uneasy seat on horseback which
afflicted him through life.

Prince Augustus, in thus tracing back the
trickles of his ancestral blood, came on a
puzzling problem – the mathematical fact,
namely, that at about the twenty-fifth generation preceding (collateral names had begun to
disappear at the tenth) he had more grand-
fathers and grandmothers than the actual
population of Europe at that date, and at the
thirtieth generation more than could have

existed in the whole world. Presently, however, even this pleased him, since it proved that mathematics, which he greatly disliked, did not contain ultimate truth but shared the fallibility of Popes. He had, therefore, less cause to be ashamed of his persistent tendency in his accounts to translate sixteen pence into one-and-sixpence, and make two hundred and fifty go to the pound. Money puzzled him; and though he liked spending it, he had a difficulty in making ends meet.

During these same holidays, which revealed to him the number of his ancestors, he paid his first visit to a Zoo. Darwin has not yet come to trouble the shallows of religion, and make muddy its waters with the hoofs of his heresy. But the Prince, on his own account, had some searching thoughts which found place in his diary:

'Yesterday I went to see a large collection of wild animals and other beings whom it is impossible for science to classify. It is very mysterious that God made so many creatures with no apparent use, and some, indeed, very harmful in their habits, and of a disgusting smell. It is also curious how like human beings monkeys can be, not only in their features,

53

which are strikingly so, but in their ways. It is
a merciful provision of Providence that we are
not more like them than we are; but I think
that we are less like them than the French,
which also shows itself in history and religion
and indeed everywhere. Monkeys seem to have
a language, but not so advanced and easy to
understand as parrots. If a parrot really knows
what it is saying, there is hardly anything more
mysterious in the world than the reason why
this is so, or how it could have come about;
because in their own native forests it must have
been very seldom that they met any European
or heard any language spoken such as they
could understand.

'Mr. Tollet would not allow me to ride on
the elephant, because we were there incognito,
and the public was not to know.'

    .   .   .   .   .

'To-day is the dear Queen's imaginary birthday; but I cannot help wishing her real life and
happiness. In writing of the King's, Mr. Tollet
said I used a wrong and disrespectful word
which I should not have done; so I hope that
"imaginary" sounds more respectful, which is
what I intended.'

    .   .   .   .   .

'To-day my religious examination took place.

54

It lasted two hours and a half, and went off better than I expected; only once or twice my attendance failed, and I confess that I felt very tired at the end of it. I hope now that I understand God better than I used to do, as I have learned a lot of interesting things about Him which in the established religion of this country one has to believe, and did not previously know.'

.   .   .   .   .

'To-day I was confirmed. I thought the Archbishop did it very well and solemnly. The King and Queen and most of the Court were there; and I hope it will have all the effect on me that it was intended to have.

'After it was all over the King bestowed on me the Order of the Martyr which I am very glad to have. It seemed a suitable occasion for getting it. It has been a trying day for me; but already I feel better.'

.   .   .   .   .

'I regret to say that I have still one great fault which I cannot get rid of, and that is the desire, if I may so call it, of doing nothing at odd moments. This is a thing which anyone going into the army must correct, as it might be fatal to decision at a critical moment while acting as its imaginary head at manœuvres, or even in a real battle.'

.   .   .   .   .

'I regret to say that my conduct yesterday was such as to cause Mr. Tollet to order me to breakfast in my own room. He had been telling me that it was most important that I should improve in my riding and not fall off my horse so many times. To which I ventured to answer that it was my own beastly look-out, not his: a most impertinent and uncalled-for expression under the circumstances.'

.   .   .   .

'The flag on the Palace is flying at half-mast to-day for the late lamented death of one of the larger sovereigns of Europe with whom some years ago we were at war; and we are also going into mourning for three weeks owing to the same cause. It is most important when sovereigns die that they should show this sort of respect for each other, as it sets a good example to their peoples in having a right idea about Kings and God's will concerning them.'

.   .   .   .   .

'To-day is the confirmation of Princess Augusta. With what awful thoughts must this poor little Princess go up to the altar to take on this added weight of responsibility consider-

ing her inadequacy owing to sex for the position
to which she appears to have been called.

'I am now able to shoot hares quite easily;
but I miss pheasants terribly; they get up with
such a noise and are always so close and unexpected. This, however, is very good training
for one who intends to be a soldier, as similar
things must often happen in an army.'

.   .   .   .   .

'It is a very odd thing that I cannot get on
with Greek or Latin; but dead languages are
of course, in the nature of things, much harder
to adapt oneself to than alive ones. Mr. Tollet
has often explained to me why I have to; but
the explanation does not seem to make it any
easier. Life is a great mystery, and especially
to think I have to do a lot of things that will
become unnecessary if I do not have to survive
my Cousin Augusta before she has time to
marry and have children. I do wish it could
be settled sooner.'

An event then follows which fittingly brings
this first series of quotations from the Prince's
diary to an end. After this we shall find a
difference.

'Alas, the time is now at hand when I shall
have to quit the care of a beloved Tutor, who

has been with me ever since I came to this country. This may even be the last record in my diary that will meet his eyes. Writing it without him to correct me will be a much more hazardous undertaking, for which I feel in all ways ill-equipped and uncalled-for. Life is a great mystery; and as we grow older it seems to become more so; indeed it is difficult to see how it can be otherwise.'

CHAPTER IV

LEADING STRINGS

By this time Prince Augustus was in his seventeenth year, and the period of his military training was due to commence. Mr. Tollet, his Tutor and Chaplain, had conveniently been appointed Archdeacon of a large diocese; and his relinquishment of a post of personal service which this necessitated, seems to have been accepted by the Prince with less regret and misgiving than the entry in the diary would indicate.

He appears, indeed, to have started an entirely new diary to celebrate the occasion. In this, for the first time, we find for a while that spelling, grammar, and expression are uncorrected; the Prince is at last writing to please himself. A notable change takes place. It begins thus:

'I am to have a gentleman of my own, who is

59

to be called my millitary guvenor, and Colonel
Carteret has been chosen. I would have liked
to have him a bit younger and with less nose;
but so long as he keeps it to himself I can put up
with it. He has his definite instruckions under
millitary regulations, and of course sometimes I
shall have to attend to them but only for certain
hours of the day for the rest I am to be free.
Tollet was aloud to come into my bedroom but
now I shall lock the door. In fact I am going
to get myself a bunch of keys on the first
opportunaty it may not be necessary but it
seems to me about time to begin to make a
change. Up till now I never had a chance.
However, if I put him in his place and make
him understand he is to stay there I daresay we
shall get on allright.'

.   .   .   .   .

'Tomorrow I have to ware my star and
ribbon for the first time to meet the King of
Saxony on his arrival my first state dinner in
fact when every body has to ware there stars
who has got them. Talking about stars I went
last night to here the Royal Astromoner give a
lecture. He said a lot I did not understand and
a lot more I did not believe and last night I
went out into the Park to look for the transits
of Venus but did not find eny. I dont think

there is much religion in astronomy not Christian religion enyway. I wonder why its aloud.'

.   .   .   .   .

'Spent this morning putting Colonel Carteret in his place he told me he had been told this that and the other about me by Mr Tollet I said Mr Tollet be dammed This seemed to serprise him He said I was not aware that your Highness had lerned the habit of swaring I said considering I had six uncles alive and in the army and four of them with the ghout was I likely to avoid it? He said no he supposed not eventually but that my swaring to him about my last respected tutor was preemature. I think we shall get on all right in time However that may be I have forbidden him to write to Mr Tollet about me or ever to mention him again.'

But after this first burst of liberty the diary falls into neglect; to the Prince, writing as a means of expression never having come naturally. When it is resumed there are signs that it is not done willingly, and presently it becomes evident that once more the diary has been installed (under inspection) as an instrument in the Prince's further education and development. What follows is indicative.

'It has been quite out of my power, partly from idolness and disinclination to write my diary for the last four months Colonel Cartaret however seems to think it is still important that I should lern to express myself grammatically and that as I so seldom write letters to enyone I had better ressume my diary as an exersise.

'I am better at my riding I now dine everyday at the King's table at 4.30. Nothing else has happened of eny importance In Flanders there seems to have been a sort of revolution for a few days but it was put down again and the King having died matters became easier. I hope the new King will do better as he is one of my godfathers.'

Meanwhile, and about this time, he and Augusta had met. It had not come about without delay and some difficulty. Prince Augustus had now been in the country for three years; but only once during the period had he set eyes on her. Then, driving by the main road to the capital from Crown Castle, on the four-in-hand coach of one of his uncles, he had seen walking at a distance along one of the bowery glades of Prince's Park, Princess Augusta and her mother attended by a footman carrying shawls and parasols. His uncle had pointed the pair out to him with a contemptuous jerk of his whip, and the remark, 'There goes the old Cat and her Kitten!'

The Duchess of Bendigo was loved by none of her husband's family; and these sentiments towards her were matched by her own toward them. While she had committed the great permanent offence of providing the throne with a female heir, whom every day of their lives they wished dead, they had been more continuously offensive in their persistent efforts to get the training of the young princess out of her hands into their own: this, in view of her future importance, they considered a family affair.

The Duchess made it hers. At any attempt to establish familiar relations she bristled suspiciously; and if the King had not been upon the Uncle's side, compelling occasional attendance at Court, they would not have met at all.

It was upon some such occasion, that the two young people first came face to face. The Duchess was for ceremony, the King was not; as cousins he told them to kiss. They did so before the whole Court, and the Uncles looking on counted it as a point scored to them.

The Cousins liked each other sufficiently

63

well. That evening they were twice partners at a Court ball, and the next morning rode out together in the Royal Park – Augustus according to habit falling off his horse when it shied. Practice had done little for him; never did he like riding or master its mysteries; apart from the hereditary drawback he had not the right legs for it; and his most earnest moments of prayer throughout life were when having to attend a review and meet salutes over a horse which had spirit. To obviate this trouble he adopted, later, the device of having all his mounts ridden to a standstill the day before appearing on them in public; that, and a low diet in between, gave the requisite sobriety to their deportment, and to him safety.

Augusta rather liked him for falling off; it made her laugh; and laughter having been wholly eliminated in the maternal training of her young life was doubly welcome to her when it came. Also she heard him swear; previously she had only heard the King and her Royal Uncles do it; in this boy cousin, so shy and otherwise uninformed, she found it rather attractive, and even at that early age he did it well.

To this meeting the Princess Augusta makes reference in her diary; for diaries seem to have

64

permeated the whole Royal Family – the age even; and later, during Augusta's reign, it became an annual family function for its members to meet on New Year's Eve and read to each other extracts from their diaries written during the year.

The entry in question runs as follows:

'I think my Cousin William Augustus, whom I have now met for the *first* time, is a very nice young person. He seems to have more *principles* than many do of his age and sex in our position of life; and indeed *some* who are *much older* and so ought to know *much better*. Also he is not too well-educated, so is easy to get on with. He gave me a very pretty pin-cushion made for me by his mother, and which I shall always value and use. I am sorry he has had to live so much in Germany, as it has made him too like a foreigner when he speaks. He does not ride as well as I do; and that pleased me, for it has given me much trouble, and now I begin to have more confidence in myself. I noticed that William has nice hands and that his nails are clean. That is a great thing in one so young.'

It was well noted by the Uncles that the two Cousins had got on well together at their first meeting. Word of it went round.

When Prince Augustus resumes his diary he makes no mention of the encounter; other things have been made to occupy his mind; the ascendancy established over it by Mr. Tollet has been to some extent transferred to his successor; but not quite. Nevertheless a diary for inspection is still required of him; and, after an interval of unrecorded kicking, he complies.

'From various circumstances I have been prevented from writing my diary for several months; but I have now come to the determination to begin it again regularly, and if I possibly can to continue it as long as I live. This will be good discipline for me, and a preperation for the army, which I am now about to enter. I am confident that some kind of drill like the ten commandments on Sunday, or the catechism and the articles of Religion at one's confirmation, is good for one – even though one may forget some of the truths which they contain later on, the habit of having learned them remains.'

. . . . .

'Went to-day to see the new Arsenal, which has been put up with great elegance. The King of Prussia is here, and they have been driving him about all day to see whatever would be

66

most likely to impress him, and for people to look at. There were great crowds in the streets and every one shouting but not so loud as they should have done for such an important person. I was in the same carriage but with my back to the horses, which always makes me feel sick. Uncle William did the honours for the King who is laid up with an attack of ghout. The King of Prussia is Mamma's first Cousin. I think he seems to me to be a very nice old man who impresses me with a certain degree of awe; but perhaps this is only because he is so deff that one never quite knows what to say to him.'

It was at this time – indeed the King of Prussia's visit had to do with the final settlement of the question – that Prince Augustus became aware of the fact that while in the order of inheritance he had just missed succession to the larger throne of his ancestors, he had been considered too near to it to qualify safely for the smaller one; since, for political and dynastic reasons, the two crowns had in the previous generation been separated.

Had his father, therefore, been a still younger son, the reversion of this smaller crown would have been his; had he been but one step the elder, Princess Augusta's claim to the larger would have vanished into space.

When this double injustice of fate was explained to him – not, indeed, as an injustice, but as a right and proper thing to have happened – the Prince had a violent seizure of temper which passed into paroxysms, and made it impossible for him to attend the state-banquet given that same night in honour of the King of Prussia.

This, coming to the ears of his Uncles, was regarded as a not unhopeful sign that here was the material they had been waiting for. And accordingly arrangements were made for Prince Augustus to pay a visit to one of them, and, meeting all his Uncles in a body, be initiated into the part which he was expected to play.

It was by a decision of this body or family council that Augustus had been summoned home from foreign domicile. For should events take the favourable turn which was hoped for them, familiarity with the language and habits of the country over which he was to rule would become almost necessary. But the change had taken place a little too late for Augustus ever to become quite native; he continued to prefer German and German ways; but he was docile to authority though slow, and had a touching conviction that what was to the interest of his family was to the interest of the world in general.

This meeting with his Uncles was a great event in the Prince's life; for the first time he found himself treated as a man. Stories were told in his hearing such as he had never heard before; male freemasonry was made open to him; they drank his health, and he theirs till he lost count of them; they slapped him on the back, and winked meaningly as if to say how much more of a man they knew him to be than he owned to; one of them called him 'your future Majesty.'

They did not tell him exactly what they proposed; but they gave him to understand that circumstances might so alter cases that, on the King's death or shortly afterwards, he would find himself with a crowned head.

To Augustus this seemed only a reversion to what was right, and he was glad that it remained in the family's power to correct an injustice which had been wrought into its life by the intrusion of outside law. He had already a vague sense that this should be so – the family acting as its own tribunal, and that here lay the remedy; but when, on one or two occasions, he had put the proposition to his tutor, his tutor had explained that it was not so. Now he had his Uncles' word for it that he was right; and he went back to his studies confirmed once more in the fixed idea, which his tutor had tried so patiently to remove, that Augusta had very much less right to the throne than he.

On leaving his Uncles Prince Augustus was told to hold himself in readiness for the event; and wondering, perhaps, a little what form the event would take – battle, murder, sudden death, or only the repeal of an Act of Parliament – he waited.

What happened within those next few weeks has never yet been recorded in history. There would even seem to have been, as the Dukes successively passed to their last account, a destruction of all family papers bearing on the matter. And this also happened upon the death, sixty years later, of the one most deeply concerned, H.R.H. the Duke of Flamborough himself.

In the official life of the Duke no mention of it is found; but privately and behind the scenes the Muse of History was able providentially to step in and preserve what might otherwise have been lost.

Not in the diary itself was any record set

down; just here there is a gap. But a week after the departure of the King of Prussia we read:

'I am going to stay with my Uncle Frederick. Colonel Carteret is not to come with me.'

This refers to the visit and meeting with the Uncles recorded above. The later visit, this time to another Uncle, when the event actually took place, is not even mentioned. The next entry six weeks later refers only to public affairs.

'Attended inspection of the Brigade of Guards going out to Candia: and to see the presentation of the new colours. Of the sixteen hundred men on parade there were hardly any under six feet, and so remarkably even as they marched that it was quite beautiful to see. Their buttons and their boots were also very bright. It was really quite an emotional display and a credit to the Army anywhere.'

At a Drawing-room, on the other hand, about the same date, he is less favourably impressed.

'Yesterday I attended the Drawing-room, and was in the Royal Circle for the first time. I was placed by my cousin, the Princess Augusta, but we did not speak, I saw her Mother, the Duchess look at me very often, which was very humiliating for me, or so I thought. The Queen was looking very well. It was a great crowd, over 2,000 people; among whom, however, there was a considerable collection of ugly ones. I notice that with the new fashions women's dresses are beginning to take up a lot of room.'

.   .   .   .   .

'To-day I received my appointment as Brevet Colonel in the Army. Thank God, I am now to be aloud to consider myself a man.'

A week later the King was dead, and Princess Augusta had ascended the throne. And meanwhile that thing had happened which the diary does not record.

To lift the veil we must go back to the visit, or appointment rather, made a month earlier for Prince Augustus at the house of his Uncle Duke James, where by arrangement all the other Uncles were found waiting for him. The event had been prepared. Here he was destined to learn constitutional history in a new and much more exciting way.

CHAPTER V

THE PALACE PLOT

WHAT the Uncles were now proposing to do
had been in their minds for a long time; but
they had necessarily been obliged to wait till
the two parties had reached marriageable
age. There had also been the hope, though
gradually growing fainter, that one of the two
might not reach it at all; for, to put the matter
plainly, the birth of the Princess Augusta had
not been welcome to them. It did, indeed,
seem a spiteful contrariness of fate, that following on nine males in one generation there had
been so scarce a supply of males in the next
that, even with death helping to eliminate
them, females had come persistently to the fore
with no accompaniment of brothers to cut them
out. Legitimacy and primogeniture between
them had played the deuce with the prospects
of monarchy, and a reigning queen was to be
the result.

73

Seventeen years ago the dire event had taken place; and ever since, the Uncles had growled among themselves like dogs defrauded of a bone. It was a noble and an altruistic growl; for this was a bone they could not share. Other bones – bone of their bone and flesh of their flesh – lay around in plenty, but for the purposes of monarchy there was no meat on them. Sons and daughters the Lord had bestowed on them, not a few. Out in the world, pressing and parasitic creatures of concealed origin, costing money, needing to have positions found for them, and taking so much more after their mothers than their fathers – which, perhaps, was as well, though the fact sometimes raised a disturbing doubt. In these there was no help to remedy the present dearth of heirs male lawfully begotten.

The Uncles had thought of legitimacy too late; their reluctant marriages had not been fertile; and so when priority of succession to a female child was clinched and made sure by her father's death, they pinned their main hopes for the first few years on the prevailing rate of infant mortality. Woman was the weaker sex; therefore, by the rules of logic, should be the more likely to die young. In those days there were no statistics to serve as a

74

guide; they now tell a different tale; but without the push of statistics on this occasion logic went to the wall, and little Augusta survived. She had measles, whooping cough, scarlet fever, escaped infection from a nurse carrying the germs of smallpox; and out of it all came healthy, and in her small way strong.

When her father died leaving no choice of heirs, his elders in the succession, tied up with unproductive wives, were getting old; and in the running, of the second generation, there remained only Augustus, two months ahead in point of time, not nearly so strong, and, as soon became obvious, with less brain, but nevertheless preferable. On Augustus, therefore, they set their hopes; and for seventeen years had played a waiting game, waiting either for the Princess to die, or alternatively for the situation to be so arranged that honours could be shared.

News that Augusta had shown a liking for her cousin had reached the Uncles, and confirmed their somewhat slow minds – damped by dwindling hopes of a more happy demise – in the direction of an arranged marriage. Obviously to keep the crown as much in the family as possible was now the best thing to do. A King-Consort, with family influence at his back, might for all practical purposes become

King. It had happened before; and the woman, the nearer in the legitimate succession, had become subsidiary.

That the Duchess of Bendigo would oppose any such proposition they well knew; for not only had she a virulent hatred for all of them, but she had in her mind's eye relatives of her own, as the Court of Naxos-Thuringia was well aware. The enraged Uncles had even heard that a scion of that House was being specially trained to qualify for the position, and had in addition good looks and unimpeachable morals.

With the danger thus becoming more imminent, they endeavoured to induce the King to impose his authority, and insist that the crown should remain where it belonged without any further admixture of foreign blood.

But the King was feeble and nearing his end; initiative and interest in regard to the succession were hard to rouse in him. The Duchess, on the only occasion when the matter was ceremoniously broached, had proved herself adamant. The Princess, she said, was as yet far too young to have her education disturbed by such thoughts, too young also to have a mind in the matter. So, with a great deal of sense on her side, so far as argument was con-

76

cerned, but with ulterior motives carefully concealed, the Dowager Mother stood between.

The Dukes pressed that the official guardianship of the Princess should be taken out of her hands; they would then be one degree safer, at any rate.

'Do it, if you can,' said the King; 'but the damned Duchess won't let you. Once she gets wind of it, she'll raise Hell, and the country too. How are you going to do it behind her back?'

That seemed to the Uncles almost a giving of his Royal assent to the scheme they had devised. Time pressed: Augustus was sounded, encouraged, primed, made – as he had never been made before – to think well of himself. The sensation was new. He did not quite understand, for he was not quite told the deed that would actually be required of him, but he realized that something very important was going to happen, and that he was to be the centre of it.

Things were at this stage when the King began alarmingly to die. There was no more time to be lost.

One of the Uncles whose house was made reputable by the invalid presence of a sweet old wife, extracted from the dear lady a wish to see and entertain just for once the Princess Augusta and her mother, before events of high import should make it difficult or impossible.

It was known that she had some family jewels to dispose of; they were, in fact, quite the best which in that generation had remained out of pawn. The old Duchess would never again be well enough to wear them. Augusta, with her expectations, became the most natural recipient for the bestowal of objects so regal in their splendour. And the hint being dropped, the Princess came with her mother efficiently on guard. Word had gone before; they were to share a room; the visit was to be for a week. The Uncles, though near at hand, were well out of sight, and among them the young Augustus, their trump card, waiting to be played.

In those days Royalty usually took a bath once a month; but the Princess Augusta, more modern in her habits, took one once a week; and (her life being nothing if not regular) always took it upon the same day – Saturday, as coming before Sunday. This blameless habit had become known to the Uncles, and on this they planned.

The course of events went easily and smoothly to the tick of the clock and the stroke of ten. Even now the Uncles do not appear. In her boudoir sits the invalid Duchess, with the other Duchess, the Princess Augusta, and one lady attendant, making four. At the stroke of ten, Augusta receives a look from her mother, the meaning of which she knows; ordinarily it means bed – on Saturday nights it means bath first and bed afterwards.

Conscious of a duty to be done she rises and bids good night. The other ladies talk on.

A quarter of an hour later, the Princess, informed that her bath is awaiting her, makes her way in modest solitude, by a short private passage, to the door – only to find that it is locked. She hears splashing within: some one else has taken it!

Offended in her young dignity she turns away. This is a badly managed household; she will have to complain. But then, in the nick of time, comes a confidential waiting-woman, plausible and smooth, full of apologies. It is the wrong bathroom; another is waiting prepared.

The Princess was then too young and inexperienced to realize the extreme improbability of there being two bathrooms in any pre-Augustan establishment smaller than a palace. Led by the confidential waiting-woman she follows to another door: it opens into the recesses of a folding screen; she enters; it shuts behind her.

She finds herself in a large room occupied by the Royal Uncles, all a little drunk, or at least well primed; with a chaplain a little more drunk, and her Cousin Augustus the most drunk of all: not that he has drunk so much, but it has had a greater effect on him. It has been done to give him the requisite fire and valour for an adventure which is to change the whole course of history; but the final dose has not yet taken effect.

Augustus was, indeed, one of those curiously temperamental people to whom half a glass made all the difference. On so much, he became merely vague and indeterminate of mind, with a feeling that what he had taken did not agree with him; on just a little more, he became commanding and heroic, fierce, voluble, full of courage, not to be stayed by anything.

His Uncles had calculated that to bring him to the fuddled stage first was sufficient; the extra glass should follow in the nuptial nick of time when deeds would have to follow words. For the reader will have clearly perceived what was now afoot: the door which had let in a maid was to let out a married lady; and that being done, the dying King would be asked to ratify with his royal assent. It did not enter the Uncles' heads – though one of them for a precaution turned the key and pocketed it – it never entered their united heads that Augusta herself might object, except timidly and conventionally, and because of what Mamma would say.

Why should she? Her only alternative was marriage with that foreign kinsman, whom, as yet, by all accounts, she had never seen. In that she liked Cousin Augustus, she was more lucky than most princesses whose marriages were made for them, not in Heaven but in the cold calculating balances of European diplomacy. At that time Augusta was not seventeen; what could she do against a whole tribe of Uncles, in family council assembled, virtually representing the King's will?

Well might the question be asked; and well was it to be answered.

The Princess Augusta was, even then, a hard-set fixed little atom of self-possession, very capable in emergency, as time was more and more to show, not on an intellectual basis but on that of a well-trained instinct. She had the knack of appropriating experience, and imposing her interpretations very emphatically on others.

She stood now in her pink flannel dressing-gown, height four feet eleven, surveying that undulating row of Royal Uncles, all slightly drunk, her Cousin Augustus not undulating, fixed, apathetic and vaguely staring, and beyond them and apart, something in clerical attire fumbling a large prayer-book, and leaning heavily upon a broad prie-dieu cushioned for two: Augusta stood composedly eyeing them, quietly waiting to be told what was the meaning of it all.

They did tell her; they managed to do it between them. Fully, faithfully, and persuasively, the whole situation was put before her: their reasons, which were family reasons, reasons of consanguinity and affection; the Country's reasons, which were prejudiced reasons, but still had to be considered; and behind these, dynastic reasons which had the King's cognizance and consent to back them; and finally – if more personal reasons were required as well – the good qualities and general suitability and presentableness of Augustus himself.

And there before her sat Augustus in his presentableness, not festively affected as were his Uncles, on whose well-seasoned rotundities drink had an enlivening effect, but sullen and depressed, feeling that he was going to be ill.

Augusta surveyed him as an inconsiderable item in the situation with which she had to deal; his weak chin hung loose making itself look weaker, his lower lip was wet, his eye vaguely apprehensive, bewildered: what could it all be about? At the very moment of nuptial presentation he indicated flatulence.

Augusta, without stir of feature, took note of it. Her simple mind expressed itself quite simply, and yet (perhaps for the first time) in that Royal formula which was so soon to become second nature: 'We.'

'We are not attracted,' she said, and turned herself for departure.

It was a remarkable instance of her self-possession and *savoir-faire* that she did not try the door to discover whether it was locked. She knew already that it was locked; she knew, also, which Uncle had the key; she had observed everything. To have attempted the door, and applied then for it to be unfastened would have placed her (though but momentarily) in a false, a humiliating position. This was a thing which in all her life she never allowed to happen.

'Uncle Frederick,' she said, 'unlock the door.'

The private chaplain, realizing, with what glimmering of sense he had left, that the game was up, having lost his place in the marriage service had found it again in the burial service, as being now the more appropriate. His mind tumbled to the routine of accustomed words: 'We brought nothing into this world,' he mumbled; 'and it is certain that we shall carry nothing out. The Lord gave, and – '

The familiar words fell like the thud of coffin-clods on those earth-bound spirits, and did not raise them. It was certain, indeed, that they would not carry *this* out, whatever else they did.

'All right, my dear!' replied Uncle Frederick. 'No hurry!' He swayed up and forward to lay a steadying hand on the door.

'Go to bed, and sleep on it,' he said. 'See you in the morning.'

He made the way wide for her, and the Princess Augusta passed composedly out, and went – not to her bed, but to her bath.

The Uncles looked at each other across the stricken field whereon lay no slain. 'Damn her!' said Uncle Octavius; then, more compendiously, 'Damn all women!' Then, to his brother Frederick, 'Why the hell did you let her out?'

'If I hadn't,' Uncle Frederick answered him, 'she'd have – ' The language of those days is not the language of ours; but according to the convention of his times he spoke as he felt; for in truth manly virtue had gone out of him. Those jolly old roysterers felt that they had been eunuched by a woman; and the indignity of it was great. She had made them to seem nonentities.

The only refuge for respect, in that assembly of flattened humanity, was to abuse the chaplain. They fell to, and began beating him – mainly with words, and ill-directed punches in the ribs. If he hadn't been so drunk, they told him, the job would have been done. Women were for ceremony where ceremony was to be, and expected the parson who married them to be sober, whatever the state of the bridegroom.

Having thus re-invigorated their self-respect, they sent for more drink. Augustus drank with them. Suddenly his symptoms took a turn; from depression he passed to violent self-assertion. In that mainly fuddled intellect one conception remained predominant; he was there to be married – and to be married that night.

'Who the hell am I going to marry?' he demanded. He had been brought there to be married; he was going to be married to somebody. Repressed youth broke suddenly into revolt; ten years of tutoring and twittering into diaries now produced a violent revulsion which six Uncles had not between them the moral power to quell. Midnight marriage, and this the night for it, had become his one fixed idea, instant, imperative. He shouted it at the top of his voice; there was no quenching him. It was in vain now that his Uncles attempted to make him dead drunk and inarticulate. The cup that they offered he spurned; it was not wine he wanted now.

The Uncles became fantastically afraid lest Augusta, in a house not very large, should hear the ravings of her defrauded bridegroom. These cries of defeat – a defeat which involved them – must somehow be stilled and got rid of.

In those days when only the weaker sex was sufficiently virtuous to reinact the fall of man, sex-scruples on the other side were small or non-existent: the woman fell for both of them. So now.

It was not difficult to discover under that royal roof of mixed menage, a young woman in service under suspicion of having 'got herself into trouble.' And such a thing having once happened, in the then social order, no reason for further scruples remained.

And so, cheap at the price, being sufficient to get him quiet, a temporary makeshift was found for him; and six months later – a date which only recent investigation has revealed – there was misleadingly born into the world a sorry substitute for one who – if begotten according to plan – would have been the descendant of kings and the heir to thrones.

CHAPTER VI

NEW RELATIONS

AND the next day was Sunday; and they all went to church, as everybody did in those days, when people were so much more religious than we are now.

It was at the Royal Chapel, where the choir wore scarlet cassocks, which in any other place would have been considered Romish and wrong. But, being not the Church's livery, but the King's, religion was not affected thereby, and consciences were unhurt.

It was the same on Coronation Day, which soon followed, when the most gorgeous copes and chasubles worn in honour of the occasion, having no doctrinal significance, were admiringly accepted even in those days of Protestant ascendancy. They gave a finish of splendour which would otherwise have been lacking.

Augustus sat with the Royal Dukes in a pew on one side of the choir, and the Princess

MRS. FITZ-WILLIAM AT THE TIME
OF HER MARRIAGE

Augusta and her mother sat in a pew on the other; and all the rest of the congregation sat looking at them, and worshipping: for though a deeply divided house the same royal blood ran through all of it.

So they met, and sat, face to face; the Princess looking in very good condition after her bath and her good night's rest. But the Duchess had a bonnet with fringes, which shook all through the service as if from the agitation of their wearer, and seemed to be saying to the Uncles and to Augustus: 'O you wicked, wicked, wicked, wicked men!' making poor innocent Augustus, who really had not been a free agent in the matter, feel very uncomfortable.

But years after, the Prince learned from his Cousin Augusta, then Queen, that she had never told her mother a word about it – a remarkable example of her self-restraint in all relations. So it was only the pendulous law of gravity which, as she moved her head, set the fringes of the Duchess's bonnet shaking – as they continued to shake, whenever worn, till the fashion for fringes went out.

One incident, which took place at that same service, should for its spiritual effect be recorded. Prince Augustus sat next to his Uncle

89

Octavius, who had the curious habit of passing
sotto-voce comments upon the forms of prayer
used in the service, as though he was then hearing them for the first time. Thus, during the
prayer for those at sea, he murmured 'Yes,
indeed, poor fellows, they want it!' He said the
same over the prayer for the Royal Family –
they wanted it also; and over the prayer for
women labouring with child he audibly
thanked God that he had been born a man;
but was less thankful for it at the rehearsal of
the seventh commandment, and while inclining
his heart to keep that law, Augustus heard him
mumble, 'Yes, yes – quite right; but damned
hard – for a man, anyway!'

This confession, so naïve, simple, and sincere,
uttered in his ear by a loose-living old uncle,
had a more moving effect upon the moral life
of Prince Augustus than all the training of his
tutors, the writing of his diaries, and the
attendance at church, which hitherto had so
wastefully occupied his time and dulled his
conscience.

Now he had had an experience, and it was a
dull one: he did not want to commit adultery.
And his jolly old uncle, with far more experience in the matter, agreed with him.

The memory of it stuck. And be it recorded

that Prince Augustus did not, in his late 'teens and early twenties – even when the way was discreetly shown him – take to himself a mistress, or live promiscuously, as did all other princes of his acquaintance of whatever age.

His manly difficulties were of another kind. He expended his physical energies in riding; and found that, with a broad saddle, specially made for him, he could at last do it presentably; and when he knew the horse well, and the saddle well, and when they both knew each other, could mount without qualms, and pass himself off in public in the proper attitude of male royalty.

His two first great public functions were the funeral of the King his Uncle, and the Coronation of his Cousin Augusta. At both he acquitted himself decently in the public eye; but found the one not more sad than the other. Indeed the second constituted the larger burial of the two – of his hopes, namely, for occupying Augusta's place.

She occupied it, he had to confess, well – even though on a small scale. To this we find reference in the diary; but he is not in sufficient spirits to let himself go about it; and the record strikes one as perfunctory. This is all that he says:

'The ceremony was conducted in the usual manner, with all the usual officials doing things; and I and my Uncles took the oath of allegiance which seemed rather funny. The poor little Queen behaved well, though the weight of the crown almost pulled her head off. After the ceremony, on the ride back, she had a sham one, made very light for the occasion, nobody being aloud to know. We got out before the end of the affair by a side door, and had time for a good luncheon before the procession came past.

'None of my Uncles rode; but I did, and the Duke of Wallingborough complimented me on it. I am sorry, though, that he interests himself in politics. In my opinion no soldier or sailor should have anything to do with politics at all, except to suppress them when ordered to do so by the government. His duty is only to obey orders without regard whether they are right or wrong. It is only on those lines that the country can prosper, and have an efficient army and navy.'

Nevertheless, now and then, he made his own comments on political events. He did this all through life; and started early, as the following entry, made only a year or two later, shows:

'As far as I can understand the Government seems divided between civil war or war with some foreign power. If they decide on the latter, I hope it will be France, which is our only natural enemy, and would be much more popular than civil war, which has always the drawback of dividing a nation, as foreign war never does.'

This seems to suggest that he had the beginnings of a statesmanlike mind; but, except when they went wrong – that is in a too-liberal direction – politics seldom interested him.

About the marriage of Queen Augusta, which came soon after this, the diary says not a word. It records a first meeting with Prince Charles of Naxos-Thuringia, and adds the significant remark, 'It looks as if the old Duchess is going to have her way.' After that, nothing; till an exchange of friendly letters with the Crown Consort (as he has now become) is recorded.

The marriage, of course, had made a further difference to what remained of his expectations; and before long that single burial of his hopes at the Coronation, had become a veritable family vault for all the diminishing chances which it enclosed. For even the high rate of infant mortality of those days could hardly hope to overtake what was now happening.

Augusta did her royal duty by the throne and the succession thereto with expeditious thoroughness. Before a couple of years were over the monarchy had two more strings to its bow; and the quiver – soon to be mightily replenished to the third and fourth generation – had begun to fill.

Over the first event the Uncles grunted their dissatisfaction; they would have preferred that she should have no children – that she should die in the attempt; and when for the first time Augusta retired from view with the whole nation expectant, the Uncles told Augustus to stand by and prepare for his accession should things happily 'go wrong.'

They did not go wrong in the sense intended; but when the event came off, Augusta had asserted her sex unbecomingly. This was a repetition of the original offence; but in another year she put matters right in the way that monarchy expects, and the Uncles had nothing to cavil at.

As for Augustus, having thus seen God in the land of the living, and the succession of Augusta's line established in two vigorous offspring of either sex, he no longer allowed his

94

spirit to faint after vain hopes; and finding himself so amply cut off from the throne, and with
nothing but his own happiness henceforth to
consider – domestically, that is to say – he disappeared from view for several months, leaving
no address; and came back from the vacation
with a wife.

He had done as his Uncles had done before
him but had done it differently – reputably,
and with every intention of making a per-
manence of it. She was not royal, or of the
peerage, or even of county standing; and he
had not asked Augusta's leave. It may even
have been the legal necessity of doing so which
had finally decided him to be illegal. And so,
instead, he had done the manly and the
independent thing, and sought out happiness
for himself without having it arranged for him.
And if, because of previous family scandals, and
to prevent his Uncles sowing their wild oats in
consecrated ground, a special law had been
secured from Parliament in the previous
generation, and if, according to that law, his
wife was not legal, and his prospective offspring
consequently debarred from the succession –
even though the heavens were to rain death on
the direct line now profusely establishing itself
– well, if so, what the Devil did it matter to

anyone but himself? Tutors, and diaries and all the dull dogs of discipline might go to the Hell they came from: he had done with them!

This spirit of revolt was brief, diaries and discipline were to continue; but it got the thing done. And so determined was he that it should not matter to anybody else, that from that day on he made or kept the matter a kind of mystery, announcing himself married (as indeed he was, if the entry of the name Williams in a country church register could be said to constitute marriage when the law said otherwise), but would never to the day of his death reveal where the certified entry might be found.

It remained a moral and domestic secret between him and his good wife, and helped perhaps to make his marriage the one romantic event of his career. Kidnapping Augusta on her way to the bathroom did not count, for that had failed as his one effort to lead a brigade into action was also to fail. In love he succeeded better than he was destined to do in war.

His Uncles regarded the episode in the light of similar things which had happened to themselves in earlier days. 'Sly dog! Sly dog!' they said, poking him in the ribs each in turn, as they came to hear of it, and also to inspect the lady; who met their roguish glances with a composed and domestic dignity which should have put them out of their rude conceit of the matter, could anything have done so.

It sent him up several pegs in their estimation. By an act of simple bluff common sense, Prince Augustus had achieved a reputation for high-spirited independence like his Uncles of old, in a way which left him for ever after with a quiet conscience toward God and woman. Thenceforth he became in his own eye and the eye of Heaven a married man; and was always able to say his prayers in the lady's company, a domestic habit which has its values; and it may safely be said, as regards that particular Royal House of queerly mixed marriages, that he made the best husband that had been known for two generations. His wife never had to hide under the sofa on his return from dinings out; and since his menage was necessarily a private one, it was also economical. As the years passed, he paid for his wife's clothes and his children's schooling without difficulty out of the allowance made to him by the nation for merely existing a close relative to the Throne. He gave no dinner-parties, except official ones in the large house round the corner where he was supposed to reside. He had also, in his private establishment, the inestimable comfort of more women-servants (the established family kind which then existed) than men-servants, and these not in livery; for his wife very sensibly wished always to live with a semblance of the class to which she belonged.

But all this is looking ahead. When the thing actually happened, when the rib-pokings were still fresh upon his person, only his Cousin Augusta had spoken the proper and moral word.

Because his other impinged too closely on her own, the Queen always made use of his second name. 'William dear,' she said, 'I'm sorry this has happened.'

'I'm not,' he replied.

'It was so uncalled for,' she insisted. 'You should have asked Me.'

'I did ask you,' he reminded her. 'You wouldn't have me: you said you were not attracted.'

'William!' She was annoyed at his simple misunderstanding of her remark. 'You are never to mention that again!'

'I thought *you* did,' said Augustus William.

'I have never even told – Him,' she said solemnly. The pronoun was uttered with

devotional fervour; but it meant the Crown
Consort, not God.

'No, you didn't,' Augustus admitted; 'but
Uncle James did. He told him when you first
had him over to arrange matters for your own
marriage. Uncle James thought it might
frighten him off, but it didn't. And I'm glad,
Augusta, I'm glad. You are much happier with
him than you'd have been with me. And I – '
He paused. 'Well I'm quite contented now to
be as I am.'

To her own relations Augusta had kind ways
– though ruling them at times with the reminder that she was Queen as well as
kinswoman. Now she said:

'Is she quite a lady?'

'Oh, quite!' her cousin assured her. 'Speaks
much better than I do; real gentry; had a
governess; goes to church regularly; says her
prayers; writes to her mother every other
day.'

That decided matters in Mrs. William's
favour. 'Then I shall like to see her,' said
Augusta; and she did.

As a belated wedding present the Queen sent
her a Church service bound in velvet, a Paisley
shawl, and a Crown Derby tea-service. And
after a few meetings, strictly private (Mrs.

99

Williams coming in and going out by a back way), they used, when alone together, to kiss with cousinly affection.

But Queen Augusta was never godmother to any of her children; she sent her nice baby-linen instead, and a cot with pink ribbons which she had sewn on herself. And, of course, Mrs. Fitz-William, as she came more decorously to be called, was never presented at Court, or mentioned there; and the public was never told of her existence, but came gradually to know.

And in later years the public service had to accept as Colonels and Generals men of quite mediocre ability to whom the name of Fitz-William gave a pass for positions which had high pay and social prestige attaching to them. And why not? Up till thenabouts was it not pocket-boroughs which made the Representative Chamber almost as trusted and respected as the Chamber of Peers; and had not the purchase of Commissions won the Nation its wars, or not lost them, anyway? Royal blood, even when privately vinted, is as good a test of quality as any of these; and these Fitzes, which are its leavings, are as good fits, some of them, as others that could be named which have been more democratically come by. Is not 'the Trade' itself run by tied houses? And what in the country is more prosperous?

Only in the matter of the name did Augusta put her foot down: it must be Fitz-William, not Williams. The 'Fitz' had become traditional; being a symbolic substitute for the French word 'Fils,' it carried with it a mysterious aroma of concealed descent. It had always been so, and so must go on. Somewhere or another there had been a Mrs. Fitz-Hubert; the 'Hubert' meant nothing, but the Fitz indicated that she must be spoken of with respect.

The Crown Consort, whose mind was monumentally ceremonial, also gave his countenance to the relationship. 'There is nothing derogatory in a morganatic marriage,' he said, 'so long as it remains morganatic.'

But he and the lady seldom met. He insisted that, in his Presence, she must remain standing, and this annoyed Prince Augustus. Augustus had even on one occasion whispered to her to sit down (only members of the Royal Family being present) – 'Damn it, Fanny, sit down!' he had said. But Fanny knew her place, and remained standing, even though she was then within a few weeks of presenting him with a son – not an heir.

Mrs. Fitz-William had indeed a tact which

qualified her for the ranks of Royalty, and no less for making a marked distinction between the second establishment over which she presided, and other second establishments which were then so much in vogue. Her Royal husband would have liked her to drive her own pony carriage in the Park; but she – noting the ladies who did – declined. Not even the presentation of a very pretty high parasol, which spired up into a whip, a frivolous and passing invention of the day, could induce her to revoke her decision. She had seen the whip also, and had noted what kind of ladies used that. Not in all her life did she ever appear before the public so as to be looked at.

And yet in all that generation of royal liaisons and marriages, there was none for the next twenty years who had looks to compare with hers, or for that matter manners either.

CHAPTER VII

PUBLICITY

DURING the first fifteen or twenty years of Augusta's reign, Prince Augustus was, next to the Queen herself, the most important and popular member of the Royal Family. Her children were not yet of an age to take a leading part in the pageants of Royalty; while producing them the Queen had perforce, at intervals, to withdraw from public ceremonial; and the Crown Consort was too foreign to be popular.

So, as the Queen's representative, Prince Augustus went the round of the country, receiving addresses, presenting colours, laying foundation-stones, opening railways, bridges, aqueducts, hospitals, museums, barracks, launching ships, laying cables, sinking harbours, attending City banquets, bazaars, dog-shows, Academies, horse-races, occasionally church festivals, and funerals. Over everything which, in that great and growing age, represented the wealth and activity of the nation he presided, hearing and making speeches.

His speeches were, of course, all written for him by his secretary; and the speeches to which they were in answer were submitted for his (or his secretary's) approval weeks beforehand. He would practise reading these answers the day previous to delivery; and so was able to read them as well as he was able to read anything. The papers always said that he did so with a clear and gracious delivery, in a voice which could be heard everywhere.

Once, only once, an incompetent secretary handed him the wrong speech; and the Prince delivered it the next day; but only a few of his audience made so bold as to think that his insistence on the importance of horse-breeding had but a remote connection with the opening of a Corn Exchange. After all it had some; and that was sufficient. Prince Augustus himself was quite unaware that anything was amiss, until he found himself repeating the same speech at a horse-show the next day. Whereupon he dismissed the incompetent secretary.

It was during this course of activity, when the popular demand for him was so great, that he became Duke of Flamborough, inheriting his father's debts as well as his title. To meet these he applied for an added grant from Parliament, on the score of the increased expense entailed by his public appearances; and this being handsomely conceded, he made his father a posthumously honest man, and himself no poorer.

Steady, plodding, and conscientious, he carried out his round of duties with a dull, heavy air of deliberation which only evoked the general remark that he had 'the royal manner.' He continued to prefer functions when he had not to ride; but whether he rode, or drove comfortably in carriages, he always wore the uniform which was expected of him – that of one or other of the regiments to which he had received honorary appointment.

When thus representing Royalty of a degree higher than his own, he found himself always attended – in addition to his military attaché or other gentleman-in-waiting – by a mysteriously unobtrusive person who went by the name of 'Smith.' Smith, never noticeable – in a dress which somehow seemed to make him invisible to the public eye, was always there close at hand – ready, waiting, observant, and informative when anything had to be inquired about.

The Duke never spoke to him; he never spoke to the Duke. He spoke to the attaché, and the attaché, waiting till Smith had respectfully withdrawn a pace or two, would tell the Duke what Smith had said.

After the Duke had heard Smith's communication, and now and then the attaché's comments thereon, the Duke would give a decision; and the attaché would make an imperceptible gesture, meant for the waiting eye of Smith, indicating either yes or no. If it was yes, then something would happen outside the programme laid down for that particular royal progress and the newspapers would report on it in appreciative terms the next day: another instance of royal kindness, condescension, or thoughtfulness – unexpected relief for the poor and suffering, half a crown for a child who had lost sixpence in the gutter and was crying over it, or an example of that wonderful memory for faces which Royalty carried with it, whereever it went.

But the kindness, the gracious thought, the memory were Smith's. Smith was the Duke's publicity agent. If in the crowd there was an old veteran of the Napoleonic wars, the Duke sighted him, and had him forward, and handled his medal, and inquired after his wooden leg, and gave him a coin of the realm large enough for him to drink the Duke's health in champagne. And this being done, the crowd cheered mightily, and the institution of monarchy went strengthened on its way.

Or perhaps there was a Free Church Conference, five thousand strong, about to emerge from a neighbouring hall to that in which the Duke, without state and unattended, was hearing the reports of Church Missionaries; and the weather being doubtful the Duke's carriage was closed. Would the Duke, for the benefit of the 5,000 Free Churchmen, who would presently be thronging the street, have the hood put down, so that he might be seen and recognized?

On this occasion the Duke said no; for he did not love Dissenters, and had no wish to encourage them. So Smith's suggestion was turned down, but without anyone knowing of it; therefore, though extra popularity had not accrued, no feelings were hurt, Smith being too official to have any.

Gradually as Augusta's growing family

NOTE. – It was from 'Smith' or his successors, I gather, that Mr. Benjamin Bunny got a good deal of the material for his society paragraphs – Smith taking a commission on it.

arrived at a presentable age, they relieved Duke Augustus of the larger part of the work that had fallen upon his shoulders during their infancy; and he became, in the general publicity line, of less importance. But then, to compensate, he had the Army, almost as his very own; and for nearly thirty years, so much had the tradition of Royal Command survived, there was to be no Minister of State in control of him.

But that glory was yet to come; and how it came, will soon have to be told.

It was while he stood so prominently before the public eye, in ways other than military, and when in the Army itself he had no higher rank than that of Colonel-in-Chief to a regiment of the Guards, that an incident happened which had an eventful bearing on his future military career. For here to the Court of Queen Augusta came on a state-visit, the great potentate of Eastern Europe, very absolute monarch of all he surveyed, on a quest for more modern armaments especially in regard to the navy, than could be produced in his own country. The visit only lasted three days, but while it did, it was a very splendid and exhausting affair. The Army was largely drawn upon for a well-staged review; and though in

QUEEN AUGUSTA

numbers somewhat inconsiderable to an eye accustomed to millions, in physique and equipment it amazed him. And as gifts, orders, and military honours were being exchanged for the occasion, it fell to the lot of Prince Augustus to be made Colonel-in-Chief of a crack cavalry regiment in the Army of his Imperial Majesty, and incidentally to receive the very splendid uniform and commanding head-dress which went with it. With Augusta's permission he put it on for the state banquet, and was complimented to find that behind his back, without his knowing anything about it, his measure had been taken for the bestowal of the honour. Not only was the uniform the most magnificent he had seen, but it fitted. It had a fine padded chest in addition to his own, and it gave the required squeeze to the jolly rotundity of his breech and thighs, without a hitch or a wrinkle anywhere. No one could help but admire him. The Emperor said to him, 'Come to us and lead your regiment in person. They will not be happy till you have done them that honour.'

It is strange how, in the inscrutable ways of Providence, a bestowal merely by way of compliment, followed by a complimentary remark such as monarchs train themselves to employ for the smoothing of inter-dynastic relations, should have so nearly led to the Duke dying a glorious death on the field of battle in an act of strategy which, though hardly to be classed as war, was certainly magnificent in its conception.

Now, as he bowed in acknowledgment of that gracious invitation, his only thought was: 'This Emperor is a fine fellow – six foot four; I am only five foot six. I wish I could add a few more inches to my stature.'

This wish was directed more especially to his legs, which did not quite come up to the proportions of his body; had they matched better, he would have been a fine figure of a man. Horseback helped him, so far as appearance went, but still made him uncomfortable.

'The Royal manner,' which the Duke was supposed to possess, was an attribute difficult to define; it accompanied so many physical varieties. It was to be found in the dumpy and the elongated, the large and the small, the fat and the thin alike; it had nothing to do with good looks or good temper, and not always with good manners; it rose superior even to physical infirmity; in one of the old Dukes it accompanied gouty legs; and one very gracious and beautiful lady of a subsequent generation, who walked with a stiff limb, had it superlatively.

PUBLICITY

In her case it was real: but in other cases, one is tempted to think that it depended rather on the faith of its worshippers than on any indwelling presence in the Being to whom it was attributed. Possibly it was the product of a shared faith, coming from both sides: Royalty believing itself to be so endowed, and the common herd, with beatific vision, beholding the endowment. And just as pragmatism in religion may be the best justification of things difficult to believe, so with regard to Royalty and the institution of monarchy, it may account for the astonishing survival into this commercial age of a breed which might otherwise seem out of date.

There is, however, one thing conducive to the Royal manner, to which all members of a Royal Family have to accustom themselves from early infancy: They are taught to walk up the centre of a large room alone. If they can do this well, they may be as ugly as sin, but where, be it two, or two thousand are gathered together, there is Royalty in the midst of them.

This is pre-eminently seen in the child Infantas of Velasquez; who, for all their plainness, are monuments of that Royal manner to which they have been bred. And though the great crinolines and the outflanking wigs may have something to do with it, proud faith has given the finishing touch without which the rest would be null and lifeless.

In the case of the Duke of Flamborough, who had no grace of deportment, and no beauty of form or figure, this Royal manner which was ascribed to him was more difficult to define or trace than in most cases. And the difficulty was increased by the fact that he ran two establishments; and in the one his Royal manner was observable by those who knew and looked for it, and in the other it was not. He would, at certain regular hours – for he was nothing if not methodical – pass up the paved garden of his official residence, as Duke of Flamborough; as Duke of Flamborough unlock, and disappear through a private door; and a couple of minutes later would enter the door of another residence – not official – as plain Mr. Fitz-William; and there – though everybody knew that round the corner it existed and was constantly in demand – there the Royal manner was not to be seen.

Was he happier with it, or without it? And where, in those to whom it has become second nature, will its final justification be found? Will they get as full value for it in the next world as has been accorded them for it in this? Will it make all the difference, in the matter of salvation or damnation, when, at the Day of Judgment, they display before the eyes of the Highest Authority in such matters their power to walk with self-possession and un-concern, up the centre of a large room – alone?

CHAPTER VIII

PROMOTION

'Also!' said the Duke.

News had just come to him of the death of the great Field-Marshal Wallingborough, who, in recognition of his distinguished services on the field of battle, had been titular head of the Army for the last twenty-five years.

'Also.' It was an embracing comment, imported from another language, which the Duke often used, and with which he frequently began his sentences. It did not mean anything in particular; but it loosened the hinges of speech for him – helping him to think.

So now, 'Also': the great commander-in-chief was dead. Who was going to step into his shoes, and occupy as large a portion of them as might, for one of lesser genius, become possible?

The country had been so long at peace, that no military reputation stood in the way. The Army was what it had always been and would

continue to be. It had its traditions, its
machinery, its drill, its uniforms, and was in
all ways a complete and beautiful spectacle.
Changes, vast and strange, were taking place
in the building of battleships; sails were dis-
appearing, steam was countering storm, a
torpedo already existed which could travel four
miles an hour, and was kept in an aquarium
as a curiosity. But on land no such changes
were happening, so far as the Army was concerned; railways were for commerce only, and
armoured trains had not yet been thought of.
When, a generation later, thought of them was
forced upon the Duke by his technical advisers,
he thought very little of them indeed, and
exulted whenever he heard that any of them
had been knocked out by a lucky gunshot from
the enemy. 'Also: you see!' he would say.

Wallingborough had re-shaped the Army of
forty years ago (out of material that had
frightened him) to win – with ill-equipment,
a poor commissariat, and a dogged courage,
which did not know when it was beaten – the
battles of his day; and he had won them quite
as much against the Government departments
which controlled his supplies, as against the
enemy. Having done so brilliantly against
heavy odds upon two fronts, and having no

need when peace came to do any more or any differently, he had kept the Army, on its peace-footing, in the traditional form of that great period to which his defeated opponent had given his name; and now, four decades later, the Army was valiantly ready, at the call, to spring to the efficiency of a generation ago.

It was a form of efficiency which had existed so long that it had become sacred, almost as sacred as monarchy itself: as sacred as the Hindu cow which, even in Calcutta, lies down to block the traffic as it chews its cud, making tram-lines a political impossibility.

To whom now was that sacred trust to be committed, so as to remain safe? The Duke could think of only two; and of the two he preferred himself.

So, it appeared later, did everybody, except Queen Augusta; she preferred the Crown Consort.

In the weeks following, very little, officially, was said in public; but much was known, or surmised. Something was going on behind the scenes – a battle of wills, the ministry and the monarchy were at strife.

The Duke carefully refrained, on advice, from going to Court – had a diplomatic cold and got himself laid up. And meantime the organs of the Press, having sensed the public mind, fell into line with great unanimity and precision – found their range, and opened fire.

With all due respect it was impossible, they declared, that the Army should have at its head one who was of foreign birth, whose very accent betrayed his origin. This, however, had not, as might be thought, any reference to the foreign birth and accent of Augustus Duke of Flamborough. The Duke's foreign birth had been entirely wiped out by long residence, by his early acceptance of native habits and customs, by assiduous military service, in which – passing from lower rank to higher – he was now of professional standing; and had also (this with reference to the second point) a fine command of military language: when he swore at his troops, he swore so well that his accent was not noticeable.

Decision hung in suspense; it was hardly a matter for ministerial resignation; but even that was whispered as possible.if, in this matter, the popular choice was not conceded.

And then – in the nick of time – came war; and the question of titular head was postponed and put away as being no longer practical politics. For during a war an army does not need a titular head – only unity of command.

And to neither aspirant for the post of Commander-in-Chief would any responsible minister have dreamed of committing the fortunes of the army in an actual war.

The only person who thought differently in that matter was Queen Augusta; she would. To her the outbreak of war – though it made a difference – did not make the same difference as it did in the minds of others. Augusta was nothing if not dynastic. She believed in God, and in the divine right of Kings, and that they were called not only to rule and declare war, when that had to be done, but also to direct its operations.

She, as a woman, could not do so; but she had a very deep conviction that – failing herself – nobody could do it so well, or so much in accordance with God's will of vengeance on her enemies, as a member of her own Royal House.

Faced by actual war and all its dangers, however, she could not bring herself to risk the precious life of the Crown Consort; but she had not the same reluctance to risking the life of her Cousin Augustus, and was willing, anxious even, – leaving the titular headship in abeyance – to appoint him *acting* Commander-in-Chief to her forces in the field for the duration of the campaign.

But though that was in her mind, she saw that it could not immediately be done in so sceptical an age. Duke Augustus had never seen a gun fired in anger, or a man fall bayoneted or shot through any part of his body; had never presided over a Council of War, or handled the problems of commissariat or followed an advance, or led a retreat. In all these matters he must, for a few weeks at any rate, get first-hand experience; and then, she had very little doubt that the Royal manner would prove itself upon the field of battle, no less than in court circles, as a gift sent from God.

So, waiving her immediate claim and postponing the titular one, she gave the temporary command, as her ministers advised, to Field-General Lord Randogger, who had seen service in the wars of the previous generation, and to Prince Augustus a staff-appointment under the High Command, so that, in closest proximity, he should learn by observation the ways of conducting a campaign. Thus, in a few months, she hoped to be in a position to make new arrangements of a more dynastic character.

This important matter of the Command being thus temporarily settled, the reader will be wanting to know against whom war had been declared, and what it was about? It had been declared, of course, upon the country's 'natural enemy,' which was no longer France. Naturalness, being the thing of a day or a generation or two, you cannot make a mummy of it; though you may at times bury it in the sure and certain hope of a joyful resurrection.

Duke Augustus, slow of understanding, had not realized that when nations are highly civilized, enemies do not remain 'natural' for long. They change: the friend of yesterday becomes the foe of to-morrow, – the foe of yesterday the friend. As at a dance, where it becomes too pointed and impolite to the assembled company always to dance with the same partner – so, in the alliance of nations, appearances and the balance of power can only be preserved by a system of continual transference; and when you have soundly beaten your enemy over one quarrel, you raise him up, under extenuating circumstances, to be your partner in the next.

So it was now; and it was against the Imperial Sovereign Ruler of the regiment to which Duke Augustus had so recently been appointed Colonel-in-Chief, that a combination of the more civilized Powers was now directing its armaments.

There had before been other combinations,

for that swing-round of the balance which is necessary to correct undue increase of power and prosperity in nations other than your own; but this particular combination had never previously taken place; and it was perhaps no wonder that the simple and slow-moving mind of Duke Augustus, in the careful avoidance of politics, should remain somewhat confused by it; and that he should actually have embarked on the voyage which was to give him his first contact with war, in the confident expectation that, by the time he arrived, the situation would have cleared itself, and that he would find as his leading opponent, *not* the gracious person who had bestowed on him the splendid uniform made to measure beforehand, but that crafty Power which always had been and, in his estimation, always would be the natural enemy not only of the country of his blood, but the country of his adoption.

And it was, perhaps, in this hope, that he packed and took along with him the splendidly caparisoned uniform and saddle-cloth, as yet only once worn, of his Ukrainian regiment of Guards, which he had been so graciously invited to visit, and thereto had engaged him-self – an engagement the fulfilment of which became now for the first time possible.

With a three weeks' voyage ahead, he hoped to have time to learn the essential words of command in the language spoken by his regiment. It is, indeed, always well when you embark on war, to learn the language of as many of the concerned nations as possible, since you never know in what direction its fortunes may carry you, or with what nation you will wish to be on speaking terms when fighting has made you know each other a little better.

As for the cause of the war – other than that shifting of the balance which, in international relations, is like the changing of partners at a dance, – no adequate cause has ever been discovered to this day; so no time need be wasted on it here.

And similarly, over the conclusion of the war – when it came three years later – nobody today could say definitely which side lost or which won. At the time, of course, both sides claimed the victory; but they were then so sick of the results that they could do nothing else; had they done so, the uselessness of war might have become exposed, three-quarters of a century before the world was prepared to accept so revolutionary a doctrine. And against that there were – then as now – the vested interests

which are the real established religion in our
present system of civilization.

But such ideas about things speculative and
remote, had no place, either then or sub-
sequently, in the mind of the Duke; and full
of simple faith in himself, and in war, and in
the causes of it, whatever they might be, he
embarked with the troops which he hoped
presently to command.

The sea was rough; the Duke, though about
to prove himself a good soldier, was a bad
sailor. He went to his cabin and lay down.

Presently he rang for his steward. The
steward appeared: did his Royal Highness
require anything?

Apparently he did. 'Also,' said the Duke.
The steward fetched it with expedition.

CHAPTER IX

ON ACTIVE SERVICE

LITTLE is told us in the official 'Life' of what actually took place during those few short months – the only time, in his long and honourable career – when the Duke was allowed to see active service, taste the joy of battle, and be under fire.

The details are officially preserved, but they are not in print. We are merely informed that, owing to failure of health, he was invalided home at the fall of winter, and became on arrival, amid loud popular acclaim, the first recipient of the medal which was already being minted for award to the whole Army later on. He was also, in recognition of distinguished service, made a general.

A part of the veil hanging between us and that holiest of holes – a pigeon-hole at a War-office – is now to be lifted; but the lifting can only be partial; for it depends mainly on the

Duke's own memory, which was defective and also a little confused, and the notes that he made from it in private memoranda, which partook of the same character.

But though strange and unexpected things thence come to light, they make one at least quite evident – the Duke had no lack of personal courage; had, indeed, from the official point of view, too much of it: though he was of precious Royal blood, there was no holding him.

His first engagement, on landing in Colchea, had been, not with the enemy but with the Head-Quarters Staff and the Commander himself. They had, it appeared, received instructions about him from the War Office: he was to be attached to the staff but not of it – never under any circumstances to be in the range of fire. No bullet or cannon-ball of the enemy was to be allowed the prestige of having laid low a Prince of the Blood, Cousin to Queen Augusta, and still possible heir to the throne.

And so, during the first action, he was given writing to do, the copying and translation of messages marked 'highly confidential' between the Commanders of the Allied Forces. But the sound of increasing gunfire made havoc of his penmanship; ceasing to translate he became translated, and with a noble rush of insubordination mounted horse and rode into the fight.

The fight was not visible, but it was there; it was one of the many engagements which took place in fog – the double fog of a low-lying marshy coast and a defective intelligence service; so that on several occasions, when they were supposed to be fighting the enemy, they were (greatly to the Duke's satisfaction, when later it was discovered) fighting their Allies. This was one of the occasions; and was, in consequence, the beginning of those strained relations which so very nearly gave the war an unexpected turn-about, unauthorized by the politicians who had made it, but highly conducive to its popularity with the Army, could it have been allowed.

Into this befogged scene of early but unconscious reversion to traditional antagonism, the Duke rode, hatless but happy – a large quill pen thrust behind his ear: met, in the Royal manner, the remonstrances of the Commander and his staff (who on this one point of strategy were in complete agreement) and refused to take no. Putting the matter quite simply, he said that if he were not to be allowed to see things for himself, and take part in them, he would resign his commission and go home. It was a characteristic reaction from that repression under regime, which had occasionally happened in the old diary days, and was always liable to happen, through later years, when cold reason opposed itself to his deeper instincts and convictions. Not for nothing had descended to him, from one side of his ancestry, the rudiments of a tail.

And that same night, when the action was inconclusively over – except for the establishment of sore feelings between the Allies – he wrote to Augusta on the subject; and Augusta, whose plans for his advancement to the active command differed greatly from the plans of her ministers concerning him, gave him her backing; writing, in the impulsive way she did when things moved her, that he was to be allowed 'to go *everywhere* and do *everything* compatible with the training of one who might presently be called to *High* Command.' She added she did hope he had some one with him to see that he changed his clothes whenever he got wet, and especially his 'poor boots and socks, which otherwise is so liable to prove fatal.'

After this he went his own way – incidentally

127

getting a good deal in the way of others; and the Commander and his staff prayed daily – it became, indeed, their devoutest prayer – that a slight wound might lay him low, or, failing that, a touch of dysentery.

As a temporary alternative they had him vaccinated; he took it well, with symptoms of blood-poisoning, and for a week was laid up with it. But as nothing happened to be doing that week he missed nothing; and was in time, on his recovery, to take a part which has never been properly recorded, in the great Battle of Fogs, where so many regiments first lost and then found themselves again, in such unexpected places.

It was, therefore, the kind of battle which specially lent itself to the Duke's style of action, which, under fire, was instinctive or intuitive rather than strategic. This arose from the fact that, in the sphere of operations, with shells bursting in front of him and guns firing from behind him, His Royal Highness developed a double excitement; when outside the range of fire, he had an uncontrollable desire to get into it, and when under fire an equally uncontrollable desire to get out of it. Thus, left to follow his own desires (which had become the only solution of the difficulty), he spent most of his time riding backwards and forwards at a great rate, first into battle, then out again, 'seeing things for himself' over a far wider range than would otherwise have been possible. And be it said to his royal credit, that the dash and eagerness with which he returned each time to the danger zone were fully equal to that with which – having sampled – he quitted it.

It was something of a miracle, that he was never wounded or captured. Twelve times he fell off his horse, either because it was shot under him, or because it took fright; seven times had his hat carried away by shell, splinter, bullet, or wind, and on various occasions lost his way and his bearings so completely that he did not know whether he was going in the direction of his own lines or the enemy's.

For this nomadic habit he became admiringly known in the ranks as 'the Flying Dutchman'; less admiring was the Commander's comment that 'if we don't get him labelled, so as to be identified at five hundred yards, some day our own troops will be shooting him. And a hell of a row we should get into for that, if we told 'em the truth about it, which of course we shouldn't!'

Of course not; in such circumstances we never do. The military machine sends home no record of the numbers shot from behind by their own side, either blunderingly or unavoidably. Yet rumour has it that once, when the real action of the day was over, a battery was mutinously exterminated by the survivors of a certain line-regiment which had suffered too much under its inattention from the rear. As a result of which affair, the nick-name of 'Dog eats Dog' was given to both battery and regiment, and a ferocious 'rag' has gone on between them ever since; for when breach of discipline becomes a tradition nothing perpetuates it so effectively as the military spirit.

Similarly it was the military spirit in the Duke which made him become a law to himself, and perform an action which might have had brilliant results – though possibly fatal to himself – had he not been recognized in time.

The Battle of Fogs, also known as the Soldiers' Battle – because the Generals could do so little in it and were obliged merely to trust to luck, and the hard grit of their men in hand-to-hand fighting, with no ordered plan to guide them, – had three fogs to justify its name; a

white one which at dawn covered the ground
to a depth of about four feet, and through
which the troops waded breast-high into position, and, had they only thought of it, could
by crawling have made a surprise movement
which would have won the battle in the first
hour; a grey one which, as long-range firing
began, drifted in from the sea, and covering
everything made marksmanship impossible;
and an orange-tawny one (compound of a
mixture of the atmosphere and the imprisoned
fumes of rifle-fire and cannonade), which came
on toward noon when the battle was well under
way. This was the most inconvenient of the
three, as it caused the troops to cough; and
the enemy had only to listen in a given direction to know from the density of the coughing
the density of the ranks opposed to them. For
some reason or other, perhaps from being more
acclimatized, the enemy coughed less. Later in
the day a breeze got up, and the fog lifted.
It was with the first lifting of the fog that
the event took place in which the Duke so
nearly immortalized himself, but was instead
taken prisoner by his own side while in
an act of apparent desertion and thereafter
permanently removed from the scene of
operation.

While the fog lasted it had been a great day for scouting parties; and a good deal of information had been brought in as to the positions of the enemy, which the Command, owing to atmospheric conditions, was unable to put to any practical use. In the main, the battle had degenerated into a slow process of grind and squeeze, rank against rank, an affair of infantry in which mere weight told more than intelligence. But about noon intelligence had come that on the further side of a certain wood lurked a large regiment of the enemy's cavalry waiting for the opportunity to make a flank charge upon any advance over the country so invitingly open ahead of them. Even the name of the regiment had been discovered.

It became obvious that the tactical thing to do was to make a half-way advance, bring the main body to a halt, and carry on in skeleton formation, under cover of the fog, in the hope that the enemy mistaking the skeleton for the substance might be induced to charge. The matter was openly discussed by the staff, and preliminary orders were given.

All went well for the start and might have gone continuously well to a glorious conclusion, had not the fog lifted before its time.

This, on the presumption that they had a sane enemy to deal with, completely dashed their hopes of effecting, in that monotonous conflict of mist and mush, one clean stroke of generalship to bring things to a conclusion.

But apparently the enemy they had to deal with was not sane. The fog lifted, making the position clear; the trap became apparent – bare, exposed, uninviting; and yet in spite of it, and into the very teeth of it, in swift jingling motion, a broad band of flashing steel, magnificently mounted, and riding as men born to it, came on the enemy's cavalry. In another hundred yards they would be within range; destruction waited them.

The skeleton formation scampered back into cover of the main body; five thousand rifles waited quiveringly the word of command. They were almost within range now, and still sanity had not struck them to a halt. On and on they came: presently – not yet – you would be seeing the whites of their eyes.

An amazed Adjutant-General was staring at them through his field-glasses; suddenly, with a jerk, and an exclamation of incredulous horror, he handed them to his Chief. A moment later an orderly was slung into motion, and an order shot down the lines to withhold fire.

To the Commander's saddle-bow a noted sharp-shooter was summoned – nay dragged by the scruff, hoofs galloping over the intervening space of ground. The Commander stooped and pointed to one ahead – riding conspicuously less well than the rest, but gallantly and with waving sword.

'You see that – blank, blank?' said the General. The sharp-shooter, telling of it afterwards, gave the General's actual words. Here it is unnecessary.

'Don't shoot *him*: shoot his horse!'

The sharp-shooter levelled his rifle; at the detonation that followed, the horse bounded and fell, and the Duke fell with him. An order to fire *high* was given; and the Ukrainian Guard, leaderless, and back in its right mind, finding itself faced by overwhelming odds, evaporated back to its own lines.

While two officers were sent forward on a confidential mission, order was given to the five thousand troops to turn right-about face. And with the position thus safely covered, the Duke in his borrowed plumes was taken prisoner and sent back under escort to his quarters; and a week later home.

Some readers perhaps may want to have this matter explained. But the explanation is, indeed, very simple. The Duke had been present when word first came to his Chief and the staff of the enemy's cavalry lying in position beyond the wood. And when, further, his own Ukrainian Guard was designated, it kindled in his system the strategic spark which till then had lain dormant. Clearly it was under Divine guidance that he had brought with him the uniform and its accompaniments – the golden spurs, the giraffe-skin saddle-cloth, and the towering top-knot, denoting his rank as Colonel-in-Chief – which had taken up so much room in his baggage.

In half an hour he was wearing them; and before the full hour was over had found his way through dense mist and wood and thicket to the head of the regiment which had so long been waiting for the visit he had promised them.

How the Duke, facially a stranger, and with only a smattering of the tongue for conveying the necessary word of command, was able to persuade the regiment to accept him, and ride gaily to its death (which was the plan he had in mind for it) the Duke's memoranda of the incident do not explain. It appears to have

135

presented no difficulty to his mind, or, indeed, to his carrying out of the project, so far as the starting of it was concerned. How it ended we know.

On paper and in textbooks, no doubt, we should be told that this sort of thing could not be done; experienced strategists met in council, were such a proposal put before them, would likely enough say the same, and turn it down as impracticable. But in spite of textbooks, and war-councils, and theorists, the thing *was* done; and though the account here given may not be strictly accurate – since it depends almost entirely on the rather rambling and confused memoranda of the Duke himself – the fact remains that His Royal Highness was sent home a few days after the battle was over, on a trumped-up charge of broken health, and with a keen sense of grievance, which he conveyed to Queen Augusta in person.

So either the thing happened, much as the Duke's memoranda would seem to indicate; or else the Duke had become, under martial conditions, the victim of an hallucination which enabled him for the first time in his life to think, act, and write imaginatively.

This at least is certain, that during the Battle of Fogs, when the fog lifted, the Army was turned right-about face either to avoid seeing something which was not good for it to see, or to avoid meeting the enemy.

It is also certain that during the same day, the Duke did put on his Ukrainian uniform, and had his horse shot under him.

CHAPTER X

THE WARRIOR'S RETURN

If, in writing this unofficial 'Life,' the chronicler has to depend on the somewhat uncertain guidance of the Duke's own memoranda, so the public of that day had to depend, with equal uncertainty, on what the Government and the newspapers told them.

The Battle of Fogs, when it was over, continued to deserve its name; for while the public was celebrating it as a victory, Queen Augusta, differently informed, was regarding it as a defeat; and with the conviction that her flouted advice would have made all the difference was very sore about it. For Lord Ptarmigan, the Minister of War, had put off week after week consideration or reply to her repeated representations that the Duke of Flamborough, having now had the necessary experience, should be given the command due to his birth and rank.

His general excuse was that he was still waiting for confidential reports from the Chief and
certain observers sent out for the purpose,
before acting in so important a matter. And
now a report had come, conveying news of a
grave reverse, but incidentally saying nice
things about the Duke; things which the Command was the more safely able to say, since he
was now well out of it and on his way home.

What the Queen thought of it all, we know
by extracts from her own diary, which has since
been published; and there we find confirmation that during the battle the Duke did something not unlike what he himself claims to have
done. As corroborative evidence we give it
here.

'Have just received the sad and shameful
news. It breaks my heart. The Cabinet wants
whipping! Had Augustus been there, in the
position to which I wished him appointed – and
not merely having to act under the *orders* of
others – this would never have happened. But
Lord Ptarmigan pays not the slightest attention
to what I say, – in spite of his oath on taking
office; and weeks ago, when I began to be
anxious and say so, he told me there was nothing to worry about – meaning that I was not

to worry *him*. How much wiser I should have been had I worried him *more*, this only proves. If I were not a woman, I would go out and head my brave soldiers myself. I learn from private despatches that Augustus displayed extraordinary personal valour on the occasion, heading a charge and having his horse shot under him: but caught a cold from the exposure which turned to the lungs, so is being sent home. This is a great blow to my hopes; and it is only to God that we can hope to look now for a happy conclusion of this most unfortunate affair. And with winter coming on, where I am told it is very severe, how my poor soldiers will suffer, away from their wives and homes, is more than I can bear to think of.'

A sense that the victories – three had been reported since the landing of the troops – were not producing any result, had begun to depress the public mind when the Duke of Flamborough (after a six weeks' delay for convalescence *en route*) returned to the country and was met as though his safe return was in itself an important military event.

Politically it was made so; the public needed cheering up; his exploits at the front were coloured large to meet the occasion; on arrival at the capital he made a triumphal entry, was entertained to a state banquet and received the freedom of the city. Also a preliminary vote of thanks was given him by Parliament; and his military status was raised to Major-General. Queen Augusta was pointedly gracious, and received him with a favour that had intention behind it. For now circumstances had given him the confidence which her ministers – more particularly Lord Ptarmigan – had forfeited; and for many hours she sat and listened while he reported to her his own personal impressions about the war, and the way in which war should be conducted.

Facts seemed to corroborate his judgments; since his departure from the front nothing had gone well. From a military point of view action had ceased; mortality had taken its place. The rigour of an exceptional winter had driven the army underground, where for months it occupied itself in growing beards, losing limbs from frost-bite, and acquiring dysentery. In hospital it died at a greater rate than it had done in battle.

Queen Augusta's relations with her ministers grew more strained; and on the wreck of so many other reputations, the Duke secured a confidence and friendship which his two matrimonial ventures – the frustrated and the fulfilled – had not brought him. For in Augusta's blood there was a strong military streak; and the military experience of Duke Augustus was just the kind and the amount to give it conviction and life. Henceforth he became, in all army matters, the only adviser she really trusted – except, of course, the Crown Consort; and with regard to him, the shaping of events ultimately proved too much for her. With that result the honour given to the Duke's military exploits had not a little to do; and Lord Ptarmigan was to get his way by artfully accepting the big valuation of the Duke's soldierly qualities which the Queen somewhat vindictively now thrust at him, whenever news from the seat of war was unfavourable.

The Duke liked his new importance as an authority on things military, and acquiesced in it; but he found a deeper and a more tranquil pleasure in the fine addition to his family which his wife had waiting for him on his return. She had presented him with twins; a form of increase which, for some curious reason, royal marriages never achieve. It helped to commend to his simple domestic mind the match he had made for himself; Nature, too, looked on it with favour. And when, just about this time, or soon after, a crown in Southern Europe was going begging, and the begging came – conditionally – to his door, with the cold calculating ministerial suggestion that a morganatic marriage standing in the way was after all only morganatic and must yield to dynastic interests – when that proposition was made to him, the Duke, speaking for Mr. Fitz-William as well as himself, flew into a great rage, and using the very proper expression, 'God damn my soul, sir, how dare you?' refused to hear another word of it.

For surely a very proper expression it was, though stated incorrectly; the Duke obviously intending to say that God would damn his soul, were he to do such a thing. And so, never giving God the occasion, he let the offer be passed on to a cousin of sorts, who accepting it became King, and made a much better job of it than he would have done.

When he told his wife of it, she only laughed, without troubling to be indignant; it was a different aspect of the proposal that struck her. 'What an idea!' she said. 'Fancy you being a King!' She looked him over kindly but critically. 'You'd have to wear a wig then,' she remarked.

The Duke was only thirty-eight, and was

already as bald as men average at eighty. He declared, in answer to the suggestion, that nothing would ever induce him to wear a wig, not even Kingship; as for her other remark, so natural and domestic and middle-class were the relations of Mr. and Mrs. Fitz-William, that he did not in the least resent the hint that to think of him as a King was 'rather funny.'

° ° He might have reminded her that he hadn't been far off it in his young days; and had he then become King no one would have thought it funny at all. And his wife's remark, and how it strikes us now are a test whether we have any more sense in the matter ourselves, than people had then. The Duke had not got so far as thinking it funny himself; but it is to his credit surely – and hers – that the thing could be said, and passed over: an expression of opinion that she had a right to hold.

It is a small matter, yet it seems symbolic of the saving grace that Mrs. Fitz-William was to him; in a lesser degree, to others also.

There are relationships which escape the conventions, without ceasing to be respectable; and for many whose lives are bound by formula, these may well prove to be the best, the most refreshing – so incalculable in their ease. Sometimes it may be a nurse, whose serviceable love for a child has retained her a place in the grown man's esteem, independent of class or education; sometimes it is a foster brother or sister; even of a valet it has been known. In the arid realms of Royalty it may well be a morganatic wife; and the benefit need not confine itself to a single recipient.

In the case of Mrs. Fitz-William it was certainly true that she provided a relationship which must have been like a well of sweet waters in a desert of sand. She was the wife of Royalty, but was not Royal herself; she was plain 'Mrs.' She was able to have maid-servants instead of footmen; to go down into the kitchen, look into the larder, and order the dinner; to go shopping, unattended and un-recognized. She did not go to Court; she did not even go into society. She would walk in the Park, and be bowed to as one of the curtsying public by those who, in her home, called her 'Aunt Fanny.' She was even 'dear Cousin Fanny' in the correspondence of Queen Augusta – on the understanding, perhaps, that letters so addressed were to remain strictly private.

Weeping Princesses brought her their griefs, when they had to make horrid marriages with foreigners whom they had hardly seen, and seeing had not much liked. And the young Princes came and talked to her (so comfortable on her comparatively small income) about the impossible restrictions of their own larger ones; also, without embarrassment or reproof, about their concealed mistresses and their impossible loves, and the deadly dullness of all the European damsels of royal rank among whom they were to search and find a bride.

This beautiful lady – preserving such stately grace, with the endearing quality of being a good and an intelligent listener – loved even to the end her foolish and irascible old man, who had once been young and for a moment romantic, and, having literally fallen off his horse at her feet at their first meeting, had remained there symbolically, during convalescence, till she agreed to marry him.

He had kept the disabilities of his rank a secret; not till they were wedded did she discover who he was. This, in a certain sense, was a betrayal; for he, being of the Blood, their union was not legal, the sovereign's consent not having been first obtained. But she forgave him that, and other things as well, at intervals; and had, on the whole, far less to forgive than the average of royal wives, who, with legal establishments, have stricter appearances to maintain.

He did not charm her, for he had no charm at all; he did not make the mistake of attempting to dominate her, for she was not one who could be bullied; but he interested and amused her, giving her the satisfaction of a vocation which had a flavour of its own. Entering her house by an unobtrusive side-door, crossing to it from the back-garden door of his own much larger one, there in quiet cover he came sensibly to earth. And though it was so quietly and easily and regularly effected, the break-away was complete. It was the one proud condition which she imposed; and if in that household the words 'Royal Highness' had been breathed in personal address to its master, the servant guilty of such a familiarity with the facts would have been dismissed. Only in the full and comfortable assurance that here he was Mr. Fitz-William and nobody else at all, would it have been possible to preserve a menage so circumstanced to the family life which its mistress determined for it.

For the Duke it was like stepping into another country, another age, another order of society. Living with her, he wore out his new clothes, or wore them into a comfortableness which

elsewhere was impossible, and spent his dis-
engaged evenings in slippers. The only occasion when any state was used was when Queen
Augusta, veiling her transit in a brougham
purged of the royal arms, would come and
drink tea with her. Then would Mrs. Fitz-
William put on her bonnet and shawl, and
going down to the door curtsy low over the
hand which was offered her. But upstairs in
the drawing-room, when alone together, they
would exchange kisses upon the cheek; and the
Queen would call her 'Fanny'; while she would
continue to say 'Ma'am.'

But there was one curious stipulation which
Queen Augusta made; when she called, the
Duke must never be there. They would talk
of him; she would look at photographs of him
in the days when photography was an event;
she would be introduced to his children, and
send them presents on their birthdays. But in
the house of his morganatic wife, she and
Augustus William were not to meet. And they
never did.

But the intimacy of the two ladies was real.
Queen Augusta would talk openly of her
family affairs and troubles: – the dull obstinacy
of her daughters, the survival into imbecile age
of Uncles and Aunts, the waywardness and

extravagance of her sons – some of them; and her absolute adoring contentment over the one she really loved.

Think of it. What a relief! To have some one in the family, and really sensible to talk to!

And all this brought about by the most sensible act of a not very sensible life; which might have been so much more sensible, could it have run consistently along similar lines the whole way.

After they had known each other thus for nearly twenty years, Queen Augusta one day expressed a lurking shadow of a doubt:

'He really did marry you, Fanny?' she said.

'He really did, Ma'am,' replied Fanny.

'Because,' continued the Queen, now that she had brought herself to speak of it, 'it would make a difference, wouldn't it?'

'Not in law,' replied Fanny.

'No; but in morals.'

It was an admission, not usual in those days that, in matters of sex, morals and law could be separate.

'Why does he keep a mystery about it, then?' urged Augusta. 'It sets people saying things. Edelbert declares that you are not married.'

'Edelbert is a young man, and likes to have

149

his fancies,' said Fanny. And the word had a double edge, as they both understood.

The Queen said no more. With what a delicacy of touch Fanny had defended the position from one who had no right to attack it. It was well known that Edelbert liked to have his 'fancies' – not only one at a time.

Queen Augusta sighed. 'I did try to bring up my children well,' she said; for this conversation took place at a time when training days for most of them were over.

'You tried too hard,' said Fanny. 'We all do. Why think about it so much? That's the mistake everybody makes. We've got to teach them to bring up themselves.'

Such a remark, coming in that age, and uttered in Royal ears – was it prophetic, or was it revolutionary?

Mrs. Fitz-William had quality.

CHAPTER XI

AN AFFAIR OF HONOUR

As the War continued, rather miserably so far
as practical results were concerned, the Government began to lose popularity; and only the
greater unpopularity of the Enemy and the
Allies, against whom it had daily to contend,
saved it from downfall.

In the Army itself the Allies were much more
disliked than the Enemy, with whom, when an
occasional truce made such things possible, its
social relations were easy and without friction.

This being a condition of affairs not good for
the public to know, it was considered advisable
to demonstrate the continued solidarity of the
Alliance by sending the Duke on a state visit
to each of the Allied Powers in turn. As this
included 'the natural enemy' with whom, like
the rest of the Army, he would so much rather
have been at war, the Duke took on the duty
conscientiously but without enthusiasm; and

151

as – lacking that – he was somewhat ineffective, his mission did but serve to emphasize, in a polite form, the cold relations already existing.

But since the visited nation was nothing if not polite when appearances were concerned, politeness abounded. Imperial Royalty kissed him on both cheeks, while thousands of spectators cried 'Live!' The most beautiful lady in Europe gave him the most perfect curtsy the period could produce; everywhere flags flung him a gay welcome; and a Marshal's baton for his hand, and a Cross of Honour for his breast symbolized the polite nation's acceptances of him as a war-hero.

He sat through a state opera performance, with a careful attaché at hand to keep him awake – because, from his childhood, listening to music had always sent him to sleep. He saw a balloon go up and return safely – which in those days was reckoned a marvel of military efficiency – and in it three live men, heroic volunteers, who also returned safely, and were decorated for their valour.

And on all this followed, for a climax, a very large and spectacular review of troops which were not going out to the seat of war, but of which – just for the occasion – it was pretended that they were.

It was in this last connection that he narrowly missed being involved in an affair which, not there but in his own country, would have led to great scandal, and brought on him the disfavour of Queen Augusta; for, with the commencement of her reign, manners, morals, and the law had all come into line, and duelling had been abolished.

But fortunately, though the challenge was given, and the duel fought, he did not fight it.

It came about from the Duke having to ride at the review on a strange mount of an appearance equal to the occasion. It was the dramatic sense of the producers that a war-hero should have a real war-horse under him; and though he had given instructions that the horse should be 'exercised' the day before, it had not been exercised enough. He had with him, however, his own saddle with its concealed grips; so though on the back of a pagan beast mercurial and frisky, the seat between was comfortable, and with luck he should be able to keep it.

And all, indeed, might have gone well, had it not happened that in the bevy of privileged ladies who formed a court for their royal mistress alongside the saluting-point, was one whose horse, an Arab mare, was more frisky even than the Duke's, and she very imperfect in her control of it. And it happened that, as the Duke rode on to the field toward the saluting-point with staff accompaniment, suddenly in his honour came a detonating roll of drums, and the lady and her mare started to dance.

Sideways, gavortingly, they chasséed in the direction where ladies ought not to be, crossed the path of the on-coming staff, and there, selecting a partner, whisked him out of it a spectacle for the Army to behold. For apparently, between her mount and the Duke's, there was an affinity, an understanding – a stable liaison possibly – which now showed itself in highly inconvenient fashion.

A second burst of the drums, and away pranced the lady's palfrey, circling for outlet, and after it pranced the Duke's larger one.

An equerry came galloping to lend an assisting hand. It may be doubted whether the lady, who by all accounts was a bundle of mischief, really wished for it; certainly the mare did not: glimpsing interference, lightly she put on speed.

After that there was no holding them; where the Arab mare led the other followed. In a beeline down an extended front of thousands of picked infantry, all in their Sunday best – a whole army helpless, because no word of command was given them to form squares, envelop, contain, or make whatever military formation might be adequate for such an occasion – down the front they rode, court lady and Duke, making for the more open spaces of the plain beyond.

The Duke as he followed was not mute; full of passion and protest he called on the lady to exercise more sacred control – her lack being the originating cause of his. And then, as she failed him, completely losing any remnant of his own, he started to curse – his one accomplishment; and not being sufficiently there in the language which she and the horse could understand, he did it in two – hers and his own.

Along those battalions of fronted eyes sped the beautiful lady, airily protesting her innocence and her helplessness, but rather enjoying the sensation she was causing to so many, and the tempest she was rousing in one.

And all the Army knew who the lady was; she being, indeed, a celebrity of her day – one whose name lingers still – of a Court more famous for its beauties than its morals: the lady, namely, who should have been (but was not) the wife of His Excellent Highness the Duc of Minorca, natural half-brother to the Throne. And the Duc, the dandy of his day, fixed in

military attendance, had to look on and watch
the diminishing spectacle as it tore down the
lines, making a horrid publicity of things, nicely
susceptible to ridicule. And in his heart was
red rage, for he knew how even here and now,
behind its stiff front, all the Army was laughing
at him, at her, and at the Duke looking not
only so like a pursuer, but like an encouraged
one. To-morrow, in spite of the censorship,
every paper would have hold of it – ribald truth
smirking through smooth transparencies of dis-
guise; and how Lutetia would laugh.

At the far end of the parade-ground ran a
plantation cut by paths. Into it the Duke and
the lady disappeared; and they did not come
back. But the Duke's horse did, whereat from
the beholding populace went up a roar, made
more devastating in its jocular suggestiveness
by the pall of silence that hung over the Army,
which, in the face of much difficulty, still had
to behave.

His Imperial half-brother said with a
quizzical smile, 'Will you not go and see, *mon
frère*, whether there has not been an accident?'
It gave the Duc his release if he wished to take
it. Unable to bear more, he wheeled up-stage
behind the saluting-point, and, little perceived,
rode off the field.

Meanwhile, an equerry from the staff went after the Duke with another horse: and he presently reappearing amid the plaudits of the spectators the review took place very splendidly according to programme.

That evening in his suite at the Palace the Duke received a challenge. It was presented on behalf of the Duc of Minorca by two gentlemen of military rank, like strawberry ice in their pink of politeness. The counts of the offence were set forth and numbered; honour was going to require a shot for each. Monsieur le Duc, he was given to understand, resented not only the situation for which he held the other Duke responsible, but the language he had employed in it. The lady, whose honour and reputation were in M. le Duc's keeping – terms were veiled, and the Duke, imperfect in the language, supposed that the reference must either be to wife or daughter – the lady had had language addressed to her which no lady should even hear. In addition to that, the Duke had so arranged matters that he and the lady had been in a wood together alone. And then, lest the Duke should not come up to the scratch, a peculiarly refined insult was added. No doubt, it was said, if the Duke had any constitutional objection to such a meeting, he had only to report the matter in official quarters, and authority would impose itself.

The Duke had his own gentlemen with him, military also, but less military in their traditions than these; for with them the duel was a decaying institution. They might sympathize, but under their own constitution it was forbidden; and they, on a diplomatic mission, were representative of government to which on their return they would have to render account.

The Duke was flustered, but not afraid. He never was. He said the thing was all damned nonsense – a mistake and a nuisance. They'd put him to ride on a bloody mustang that hadn't been broken and he was not going to apologize for it – not to Monsieur le Duc anyway. And the military gentlemen bowed with all ceremony, and would convey to Monsieur le Duc that statement, and stood awaiting further instruction.

The Duke, very properly, told his own gentlemen to arrange the matter and report to him. He left it in their hands entirely.

The plenipotentiaries withdrew, and confabulation began; and presently there was toing and froing between them and the Duke, in the hopes of securing an arrangement; for though they posed as men well accustomed to such affairs, they were shaking in their official shoes. The Duke, they knew, was no shot; and they inquired circumspectly, whether if the Duke undertook to fire in the air, his opponent would undertake to fire in like fashion.

The two others rose, bowed, and said they could undertake no such conditions. So, with that hope eliminated, the conference was resumed. Would they admit that the Duke had used words which were not seemly, used in a lady's hearing and in the hearing of an army? The inquiry was reported. The Duke said, for his part, that the language he had used was not to Madame but to her horse; and that if it was in Madame's hearing, it was from no wish on his part. The wish was hers.

This did not satisfy.

The Duke, conceding a point, said finally, 'I am willing to apologize to Madame la Duchesse for having addressed words to my horse in her hearing which she imagined to be addressed to herself.'

But this did not go far enough. It was not only for what he had said in the lady's hearing that satisfaction was demanded; but for having galloped off with her alone in the presence of the troops. And let it be understood – to be quite correct – (this at the conference of repre-

sentatives) that Madame was not indeed
Madame la Duchesse, but one nevertheless
whose reputation M. le Duc must necessarily
protect as much as if it were his own.

At that the Duke's plenipotentiaries felt as
drowning men whose feet have touched ground.
Here was hope; morality came to their aid. It
would not, they said, be possible for the Duke,
officially – representing a moral nation, to be
involved in an affair of honour which had those
relations behind it. It could not be done.

Hearing this, Monsieur le Duc's emissaries
elevated their four eyebrows, and smiled in-
credulously. Was it not true, then – were they
misinformed – that the Duke himself had
similar illicit relations with a lady who was not
legally his wife? It was no use then for the
Duke's representatives to argue that there was
a difference, nor did they attempt it. The fact
stared: the words 'illicit,' 'illegal' governed the
situation. They said that they would com-
municate further with the Duke, and in course
of time let the other side know. On that the
plenipotentiaries parted.

But the Duke's gentlemen did not go immediately to the Duke. Instead they held a
long and agitated conference by themselves.
The next day the Duke would be leaving the

country to fulfil the rest of his diplomatic engagements. And suppose the Duke should be unable to leave and the reason for it should come out? In argument, their case for terminating the affair on moral grounds had suffered disaster; the other side was unhappily too well-informed. But the objection remained as morally insuperable as ever; the thing must not happen. They almost decided to go behind the Duke's back and inform the authorities or even the Duke's host, so as to get the thing stopped. Instead, they finally decided to bring into consultation the detective service, which Royalty always carries with it wherever it goes. And the service, an adept in secret ways and primed with strange knowledge, assured them with unruffled countenance that the matter should be arranged; as far as the Duke was concerned their argument was to hold good; according to the discretionary power he had given them they should advise him that on moral grounds the affair was over, and the Duke would be satisfied: as for Monsieur le Duc, he would have to be satisfied in a different way; since he wished it, the duel should be fought; and for that the service of seconds would be required. And then, very confidentially, the detective service proceeded to explain.

A child blows upon a watch, and it opens, revealing the works. And it must be with a similar wonder that the lay mind, when it has touched the right button, has suddenly set before it what is always going on under cover in the wheels within wheels of modern government, – the unimaginable devices by which public appearances are preserved.

The Duke's Imperial host had recently been made the object of a bomb which had, instead, killed by mistake his coachman and two horses. And information had come to the Prefecture of Police that another bomb was to be expected during the Duke's visit, at a certain time and at a certain place. But though thus forewarned and able to take all due precautions, there was a reluctance to allow the Emperor and his Royal guest to run any risk of things not going according to plan. Therefore, for that occasion – highly paid no doubt – substitutes had been provided.

The Emperor's substitute already existed – a permanent post in the secret police service, about which the public hears little: and the Duke, then on his first visit, was not so well known as to make personation for a single occasion difficult.

And so the matter had been arranged; and

in the recesses of a bomb-proof carriage, well padded against the off-chance of mishap, had sat two highly strung members of the secret service, emphatically earning their pay as they faced the momentous possibility which did not, however, go off. For police precautions had proved adequate, and the bombs never quitted the hands of their throwers but into the safe custody of the police: and the whole thing so quietly, quickly, and easily effected, that the applauding public knew nothing whatever about it, nor were the papers told anything.

Thus no untoward incident had happened to disturb the political harmony of the Duke's visit. And then, the very day after, this other untoward incident *had* happened, involving not political but personal complications, and those unfortunately of a kind which brought out racial differences just when racial harmony was the thing to be emphasized. And the Duc of Minorca was difficult – unmanageable at the best of times – proud, jealous, thin-skinned, and vain as a pride of peacocks: and now, stung to madness by the ridicule of an Army on parade, was there any holding him?

Well, well, it was a thing which might have caused trouble at the time had satisfaction not been given. The Duc of Minorca is in his grave now, so the matter can safely be told. The affair came off, according to arrangement, in an exchange of four shots, which by careful manipulation had no result; but our Royal Duke knew nothing of it – nothing whatever. All he knew was that, on moral grounds, his seconds had called the affair off; and he, hearing their explanation, had acquiesced without propounding the parallel argument, which indeed never occurred to him. And so, while in the cold morning twilight, the lethal compliments of honour were being exchanged, the Duke lay innocently sleeping in his bed; and only after returning to his own country did he hear, by a sheer fluke, how behind his own back he had fought a duel over a matter which morality had said was not to be his affair.

He was, of course, very angry about it – angry with a proper and manly resentment that anyone else should have interfered, where bullets were flying, to take on the chances of those meant for him. And presently the annoyance of it going to his head, he sat down and wrote in his private memoranda an account of the whole affair, and of the duel, as though he had actually taken part in it.

CHAPTER XII

A PERMANENT PROMOTION

THE prowess imputed to the Duke, for the feed-
ing of the popular mind in the doldrums of a
war that had lasted too long, served a more
permanent purpose when the war was over.
For here, in the Royal Family itself, a military
reputation had been established; and the post
of Commander-in-Chief was still vacant. Too
late Queen Augusta discovered that she had
allowed points to be given to a rival nomination
which she could no longer seriously oppose.
The principle of Royalty in the place of
supreme command was now conceded to her,
while force of circumstances – ministerial insistence, popular acclaim, compelled her choice
to fall on one, less personally loved and trusted,
whom the baptism of battle had not merely
naturalized to the soil of his adoption but made
native.

Political scribblers, making much of a conflict which in its last phase had dwindled and become small, greeted the announcement with a pæan of triumph – the triumph of the native, and home-grown product over the foreign.

In the textbooks of history the incident is passed over and forgotten; but it lighted a spark in its day; and among the Duke's papers – the records which he kept so carefully, year in year out, of his successful and sedentary career – is preserved an old broadsheet, price one penny, testifying to the popularity of his appointment at the moment when it was made public:

'Come, bear up, my Country, and banish all
    grief!
Gallant Flamborough is now your Commander-
    in-Chief
For he is a soldier; he's got the idea.
And he fought like a Trojan in Caucus Colchea.

The Consort was never the man to our mind;
And that is the reason we've left him behind.
He was never cut out, 'tis the Nation's belief –
The Crown-Consort, I mean – for Commander-
    in-Chief.

At shooting the Consort has not got a notion,
But Flamborough boldly went over the ocean,

A PERMANENT PROMOTION

He fought on the Heights, and commanded the
    line,
And knocked down the enemy ten at a time.

With politics Flamborough has nothing to do;
He knows how to fight, and to hold a review.
But the Consort, at politics taking his try,
Goes putting his finger in everyone's pie.

For commanding an Army the Duke has the
    head;
To the life of a soldier long years was he bred.
So fill up a bumper, and cry with relief,
"Here's a health to our *Native* Commander-in-
    Chief." '

It is not great poetry – poetry written on
national occasions seldom is; but it helps to
show how the unpopularity of one public character may promote the popularity of another,
and, as in this particular case, enable a partial
qualification to become positive. For here,
before reaching the age of forty, we see him,
to the sound of popular applause, attaining the
highest possible position in the profession imposed on him by birth, and with greater
responsibility for the military machine – on
which far more than on the established religion
the Nation depended for its salvation – than

any other man alive. His qualifications: birth, and a mind which made up for its lack of intelligence by a lively faith in what may best be described as military fundamentalism – the verbal inspiration of drill, discipline, Army orders, courts martial and all causes whatsoever which ever did or ever should carry the country into war.

With these infallibilities in the forefront of his beliefs, he put the remainder of his trust in God, and swore by Him with great gusto and satisfaction in the hearing of the whole Army, whenever occasion required; and, since he conceived the government of God – the best of all governments – to be the same yesterday, to-day, and for ever, so for the government of the Army he made that his ideal; and in politics also was so consistently conservative that the only innovation he ever voted for in his whole life was the removal of one of the prohibited degrees of marriage which stood in the way of a certain family arrangement, dynastic in character, for the second espousals of a highly desirable princely widower, who was then going begging.

And since a mind of such conservative principles tends merely to mark time, by setting firm heels to ground and letting the rest of the

world go by – and after it, if need be, the deluge
– since such a mind does not go out of its way
to make events, its record is bound now and
then to be uneventful; and the biographer,
whose sole aim is significance, comes upon gaps
which there is no filling. So now with this life,
of which so much is known, yet so little worth
telling.

The official 'Life,' published within a year or
two of the Duke's death, made all seemly effort,
as such publications are bound to do, to appear
consecutive, and to extract from eventless years
the blameless colours of constant devotion to
the public service. Like the chest of a life-
guardsman on parade, the record has been
padded to make the proper and expected show.
But this narrative, more veracious and to the
point where any points are to be found, makes
no pretence to be full or consecutive; and
where nothing worth recording took place –
sometimes for several years in succession – it
bluntly leaves a gap.

The Duke is a momentous figure in the
annals of his country, not because he kept pace
with the moving times in which he lived, but
because, like a monument, he stayed sedentary.
And by his sedentariness he kept sedentary,
steady, and traditional the great military

organization over which he ruled. By this, though not intending it, he once did his country great service. It was whispered at the time, it may be said out now, that when, on a certain occasion, the Government was about to adopt a belligerent attitude, and challenge the designs of a first-rank Power, the discovery that the Army was in fact the Army of a previous generation, and insufficient unto the day and the evils thereof, that discovery provided by the Duke had the beneficent effect of heading it back into a more pacific policy. And so, when all is said and done, since on that occasion the Duke preserved his country to peace, for that at any rate he deserves a statue. But not for that was the statue given him; nor was the Duke even allowed to know of it. Instead – without true reason stated – he was super-annuated, shelved, retired, dismissed in a blaze of honour, with banquets, blare of trumpets, and roll of drums, and his poor old heart broken.

But all that did not happen for forty more years to come: and it is with the intervening years, so eventless and unimportant, that we are now concerned. During that period it is not the history of an Army that will engage our attention; that we shall find waiting for us at the other end, with all its buttons intact, and its appearance preserved; and only a few odd corners of its traditions battered or knocked off, where the Duke's sheltering wing was not big enough to protect them. What remains for record is more personal, and the diary must once more be our guide. In it, during the following decades, we read of the termination of Augusta's married life, the maturing of her large family, and of his own less large; the 'solemn entry' of royal brides amid 'enthusiastic cheering'; of ceremonies well got through, of state visits received and returned, of funerals 'going off' (like guns) 'without a hitch.' The phraseology always the same, the comments, so long as things happen as they should happen, as regular as a row of buttons. On every occasion the behaviour of Royalty and populace alike was the best possible; he moved in an environment of wheels that had been well oiled: that was his world. But now and then came a snag, and at once everything went topsy-turvy; any disturbance of order, or change of taste even, seemed a precursor of revolution.

We get an instance in the popular reception of the Liberator Badigaldi, who just then was touring Europe after the freeing of his nation from the foreign yoke. Then, to the Duke's mind, the enthusiasm of the people became 'madness.' Here are extracts:

'It is really too ridiculous the way that people behave over a man of such low antecedents, and very disgusting, I think. . . . The ridiculous fuss that is being made about Badigaldi is truly melancholy, and will, I fear, have very ill-effects on our relations with foreign powers. . . . The Badigaldi fever still rages. People actually rise from their seats when he enters the theatre; and were it a church would probably do the same. Luckily he is no church-goer, which shows the kind of man he is; and a danger to have anywhere. . . . Yesterday he arrived at the House of Peers during a sitting. We paid no attention, though it was the Prime Minister who brought him. He was wearing a red shirt, and over it a grey mantle, very eccentric and exceedingly uncalled for in such surroundings. If we dressed our Armies in that fashion where should we be? . . . The papers say that he dines to-night with the Prime Minister. This is quite deplorable. To see such a man treated like Royalty, even by those who ought to know so much better, makes me wonder what the country is coming to. I only hope I shan't live to see it.'

A PERMANENT PROMOTION.

A few years later came a case touching discipline in the Army, when the law presumed to interfere with the judgment of a court martial, which had sentenced to imprisonment a Lieutenant who, while saluting with military correctness, had refused to take the proffered hand of his Commanding Officer.

'The dreadful news has just reached me,' wrote the Duke. '£200 damages! a most singular and unwarrantable verdict, very prejudicial to discipline; and given by a civilian jury is, I regard, an insult to the whole Army, and ought to be stopped by Act of Parliament. If a junior officer is to be allowed to show his personal feelings (and his wife, I warrant, no better than she should be) what is the Army coming to?'

In the year following comes reference to a famous horse-race:

'Town very much agog, I hear: "Turnip," a rank outsider, having got home against big odds; and Paystings, who has just run off with the owner's wife, is said to have lost nearly £100,000 and will have to go bankrupt. Gilpin, backing his own horse, has taken £140,000: and Colton and MacVitie between them are reckoned to have won over £230,000, which is really too awful to contemplate; for what woman is worth it? Paystings really ought to have known better. It makes me very thankful that my distrust of horses has kept me from putting my money on them. It's bad enough to be on them oneself. Life is a great mystery.'

Public luncheons and banquets are frequently mentioned, and the food is always commended. Indeed, if one may judge from the diary, the Duke never had a bad dinner; but in his fiftieth year begins to encounter indigestion, and later comes gout.

Each of his birthdays is recorded as 'a very serious matter for reflection': 'though I have still much to be thankful for,' he adds on one occasion, as though 'serious reflection' were something of a nuisance.

In his fifty-second year he records 'with shame and indignation' his country's failure to embark on a war which he considered to be good for it. It is one of the rare instances when, allowing himself to think and write as a politician, he condemns the Government in severe terms. This is the more remarkable in the face of his dictum when matters are the other way about – and the Government decides not for peace but for war. Only, apparently, when it chooses war, does it rise above criticism. This we find expressed not in the diary, but in a speech made at a regimental dinner, where it was received with great applause; but only a modified version found its way to the Press.

'To question,' he said, 'the motives, or wisdom, of your country when it is intending war, is indecent and not to be tolerated; and to do so when it has gone to war is damnable. As for people and politicians who start criticizing the generals in the Field, I'd shoot every damned civilian who does it, and I'd turn out every damned Government.'

Terrific and explosive when on parade, of the Army in its campaigns, he shows himself a lenient critic, not expecting too much, or unduly censoring the mistakes of those – mostly his personal friends – whom he has placed in authority. Thus during a small outlying war, as he reads the despatches sent home and makes marginal comments thereon, he does not expect this weapon of his own polishing to be better than it is. Efficient within limits, and requiring no change but only a little experience to keep it in condition, it wins a battle which on paper looks well; but having captured the enemy's guns it leaves them on the field for the night,

175

and during the night the enemy come and carry them away with a few others thrown in. On this he comments mildly that 'it was very unfortunate, and ought not to happen again.' And when, with the recapture of the guns six months later, the campaign ended, as it would have ended then, he, having so brilliantly organized it from home with marginal notes of similar efficiency and quality, received for his services the Grand Military Cross, and was made personal Aide-de-Camp to the Sovereign.

Mingling music with his military duties, as a thing which must occasionally be attended to, he goes to the opera, and for the first time in his life hears what he describes as 'one of Wagner's incredible compositions.' 'I suppose,' the commentary continues, 'he knew what he was doing at the time, though perhaps not afterwards; but whether God Himself did, or anyone else, I have much reason to doubt, judging from myself, for I couldn't even sleep through it, though I tried.' Music which the Duke could not sleep through must, indeed, have been of a portentous character.

The next day he comments unfavourably on the useless exploitation of balloons for public entertainment.

A PERMANENT PROMOTION

'Saw a Frenchman make a balloon ascent on a trapeze. I thought it a most unpleasant sight, as well as foolish and useless. Balloons may be useful in war for military observation; but one can't do that on a trapeze. This balloon was not filled with gas, but the internal air was exhausted by a fire lighted within, and as the fire dies down the excluded air rushes back into place, with a great risk of bursting itself, I should say. Things of such a dangerous character should belong only to the Army, and be kept secret.'

About this time a primitive expedition into a tropical region of swamps and jungle causes him annoyance. He sees no glory in it, nor is it the sort of thing his Army has been trained for.

'This Tishatee war is very annoying,' he writes. 'I grudge my brave troops going into such a climate, where the native habits are also very disgusting. It means also an entirely new sort of uniform which is very disturbing to an Army's morale, and a thing which ought always if possible to be avoided.'

The first decade of his command was hardly over when criticism of the Army's administration began to make itself heard, first in the Press, then in Parliament; and from that time on it was a recurring annoyance; an additional annoyance being that the Government refused to treat it as a form of civilian insubordination which ought promptly to be put down as soon as uttered.

On a motion in the House of Representatives to make tenure of the High Command a terminable appointment subject to the War Office, 'so as to make available the best administrative talent, and the most recent military experience acquired on active service – permanency of tenure not being conducive to efficiency in the Army or confidence in the public mind' – on that motion, with its reasoned terms of implied criticism, he comments sharply:

'You might just as well say permanent monarchy had the same bad effect, and better for the church to have Archbishops running in and out like rabbits. And where would religious discipline and sound doctrine be then? Jacks-in-office, in and out with every new wave of opinion, is what they want! What in the world are we coming to? Talk like this leads men's minds to revolution!'

Even a transference of the Staff to new and larger premises afflicts this conservative mind.

'Went to-day to my new rooms at the War Office, where all staff-work in the future will be transacted. It was like saying good-bye to everything, and a great wrench. These attempts to undermine my position and upset tradition are very sad; and to have ministers running in and out for interference which they call consultation is what I am going to find it very hard to put up with.'

Then, two days later:

'Very difficult, I find, to concentrate one's mind in the new office. Bookshelves all different; nothing anywhere as it used to be. Even the bell in a bad place for getting at, and the coal-scuttle on the wrong side – most distressing. What the Army most wants is to be left alone. Civilians haven't the disciplined mind; and when they talk of "economy" it just means making the Army take a back seat, and the country knuckling under to people and places like America: and a pity, I think, that Columbus ever discovered them!'

In this mood of depression he comes to his fifty-sixth birthday, on which (twenty years

before his compulsory resignation) he writes –
with the shadow of the coming event already
over him: 'So old, and so many years since I
started in the Army. Alas, how soon one
approaches the end of one's career. I feel this
daily more and more.'

'An excellent dinner' is mentioned three days
running. Gout follows.

At the age of fifty-nine gout had settled a firm
hold on him, and he walked with the aid of
two sticks. He now rode only on ceremonial
occasions of a military character, often with
great pain. He attends a Royal Review in the
rain, when his Sovereign – though enjoying it
herself – shows consideration for his infirmity:

'I had my waterproof on by Augusta's permission: but wet through all the same before it
was over. Reached home at six: had hot bath,
brandy, and bed. Haven't been so wet and
miserable since I was on active service. All
which makes one feel how time is getting on so
much faster than one ever wished or expected.
The Queen has kindly sent to inquire how I am;
but as I don't want it known I have answered
accordingly.'

In compensation for this drenching he received the next day the Order of St. Swithin. Thus, if the life of a Commander-in-Chief was strenuous and not unattended by danger to the constitution, the rewards were proportionate. Indeed it became difficult toward the close of his days to find any new honour that had not already been conferred on him.

But though he valued honour, he valued Royalty more. Royalty for him stood equal with religion, and indeed formed a part of it. As the rainbow brought spiritual consolation to Wordsworth, so to this scion of Royalty did that rank into which he had been born, bring consolation and assurance like a sign set up in the Heavens of God's mercy to man.

To a member of the Royal Family came dangerous illness. When the danger had passed the Duke was able to look upon the people with new eyes. Royalty had once more proved itself a thing of divine dispensation.

'The loyalty displayed by the entire Nation,' he wrote, 'is sublime, far more than I should ever have believed, and gives a nice knock to the Republican movement which up till now has been hoping to get things its own way. For this we cannot be too thankful; Heaven has sent us this experience for our good; and all their calculations the other way have been finely upset.'

This kind of belief in the order to which you belong may also be regarded as a dispensation of Providence, making Royalty interesting even to itself. But if ever the belief goes – what will happen to monarchy?

Perhaps nothing: for, after all, there have been infidel Popes; and similarly a King might secretly believe in republicanism, and yet continue to reign; just as there are Conservatives whose main hope in going to church is not for life in a better world, but only for the stabilization of a system which suits their interests in this, and which institutional religion helps to keep alive.

CHAPTER XIII

HIGH CALLINGS

THAT the Duke was conscientious, punctilious even, in the performance of his duties toward Royalty has by now been sufficiently demonstrated. So conscientious indeed, that in the present writer's search through a record extending over fifty years, in addition to personal observation, only one solitary instance has come – one cannot say 'to light,' since the close darkness officially designed for it still covers it – but within reach of private knowledge; when he refused – refused absolutely – to do what the good of his country required of him. And the truth of it can be guaranteed, the writer having had special opportunities of which, though he makes no boast, he has made use.

How far one is to attach blame to that refusal, depends largely on the view one takes of what can rightly be required of the individual in the interests of the community he serves.

What right has that individual to conscience or to self-respect, when the State demands their sacrifice? It is quite settled in the minds of all good citizens that the individual has no right to a conscience when called on to contribute to the casualties of war, or pay taxes for purposes he disapproves. Similarly, the man who resigns his soul to military or naval discipline, must go 'on the knee' if bidden by his commanding officer, even though the order is insultingly given to satisfy personal spite. In such a case self-respect must not exist: if it does, he will be collared and court-martialled.

Has, then, a high servant of the State any more right to refuse an act hurtful to his self-respect, or taste, or prejudice, when the State sees good to ask it? Do these considerations rule out conscientious conformity?

In the matter about to be revealed, the Duke, very much of a gentleman, but with all the prejudices and limitations of a gentleman, decided that they did.

It happened thus. The newspapers had broken into large head-lines over the approaching visit of a certain dusky potentate, with whom an 'equal treaty' of amity and free commerce, for the opening-up of the vast resources of the country over which he ruled, was in process. Incidentally, we have to admit that, not long after, the said country was annexed for the imperfect fulfilment of its obligations, and the monarch himself removed from the throne, to die in exile and captivity.

But at the time of his coming, he was still independent and potentially troublesome, a ruler of war-like tribes, and provokingly suspicious of what the peaceful penetration of civilized commerce might ultimately lead to. And since he was coming in person to make quite sure that the friendship offered had no ulterior designs behind it, it was extremely important that he should be personally satisfied.

That being the position, it was discovered, on the very eve of his arrival, that the one and only thing which would convince him of the bona fides of a Christian power, and that its treaty of equality and friendship meant actually what it said, was the ancient and sacred ceremony of nose-rubbing.

This act, when performed by equals of rank, – sovereigns, or their representatives, princes of the Blood, had in the dominions of the Negus of Bessarabia, so sacred a significance, and behind it so divine a sanction as to make breach of faith thereafter impossible. Failing that, there would always remain a doubt.

When Queen Augusta heard that for the
ratification of a treaty which had great and
immediate commercial interests behind it, and
– looming large but more remote – even greater
political interests behind those; when, for the
conclusion of that treaty, she heard that a black
and bejewelled Negus would require to have his
nose rubbed, she determined at once that
though, as an act of State, it must be done,
the doing should not be hers.

As sovereign she was prepared to do great
and strange things; but just as the complexion
of her religion forbade kiss of the ring or any
other implied homage to the Pope, so the complexion of the Negus forbade contact between
his nose and hers. But since, she understood, a
Prince of the Blood appointed for the purpose,
would do equally well, she appointed the Duke
of Flamborough, without previously consulting
him, to be her plenipotentiary in the matter,
and convey – through the nose – that assurance
of his country's good faith which the Negus was
seeking.

The Duke had already been deputed to be
the Queen's representative, and meet the Negus
on his arrival; but it was only on the eve of the
event that the ceremonial details were laid
before him to be gone through, memorized,

and made easy of performance by rehearsal with a high Court functionary proxy for the occasion. These included and had for climax the nose-rubbing by which, on fleshy tables, the treaty was in effect to be signed.

Said the Duke, on hearing of it, 'I'll be damned if I do!' said also with what effusion of blood he would be damned. And in spite of all the official persuasion brought to bear, and even the awful threat that Queen Augusta might have to be told of it, he remained undamned and obdurate.

What, then, was to be done? Was the ratification of the treaty at the last moment to be jeopardized, and the very reason for the Negus's coming, with all the suspicion and disappointment this must entail, be cancelled? No; secret diplomacy, like the secret police, has its ways for getting round the acts of God and the gentlemanly scruples of men, and can, when necessary, descend to queer expedients for the salvation of its policies.

Possibly it knew what, in a case of like difficulty, the secret police had done when, for state reasons, a substitute had undertaken an appointment made for the Duke. Where there is more mystery than imagination, history tends to repeat itself: tricks that have not been found

out can be played again. So once more the
trick was played; but this time – not behind the
Duke's back, he knowing nothing of it, but with
the Duke's consent.

There was at that time exhibiting himself
before the public, a music-hall comedian with
a marvellous gift for make-up in the likeness of
his betters – the great and famous men, and
sometimes the women also, who adorned the
society of that day: a gift which he had recently
used with a daring the censor had had to re-
press. Now it was suddenly remembered with
what verisimilitude, in cocked hat and plume
and with artfully shortened legs, he had made
one of those caricatures recognizable, nay, in-
distinguishable, though with all the dignity
left out. And so, very secretly, and expedi-
tiously, and expensively, – and for the occasion
only – the censorship was removed; and on the
day, and at the hour, to the minute, when the
Royal train arrived at the place of meeting,
the Duke remaining within behind closed cur-
tains, there emerged a facsimile, so close in all
particulars – dignity and the Royal manner
included – that nobody in all the cheering
crowd discovered the trick that was being
played on it; nor did the Negus when his nose
was rubbed by a nose slightly rouged for better

MRS. FITZ-WILLIAM
At the age of 40

impersonation of the original; nor did he, when finally seated in the train with Royalty's genuine article beside him, discover that any substitution had taken place.

And so the Negus found faith in the rub of a comedian's nose, and the treaty was signed with satisfaction to both sides; and when later he rebelled protestingly against the inequality of its interpretation in practice, it was the Negus, with a very sore nose, so to speak – and not the treaty – who was abrogated and set at naught as though no sacred levelling of nose-rubbing had taken place.

Of course, as no harm came from it to the fortunes of his own country, the Duke's refusal to play his appointed part in lulling the Negus to a false security did not greatly matter. But it was one of the few instances in his life when character, coming uppermost, asserted itself against the main creed of his being. And when it did so there was, one feels, a certain rough dignity about it, a suggestion of common sense which might – to the upsetting of imposed rules – have occupied a larger part in his composition had the circumstances of his life made it more practically possible.

In a later encounter with a potentate of less barbaric race, and more splendour of personal

adornment he had easier relations. Oriental
alliances had become the vogue, when the Shah
of Pershastan arrived in a blaze of diamonds
such as had never been seen before outside a
jeweller's window, in a collection not for sale,
on the person of a single individual. His
plastron of diamonds commanded great crowds
and almost greater popularity; and though he
brought with him none of his wives, their place
was taken by a mysterious little being with
lustrous eyes, whom the newspapers (under
instruction) described as his Astrologer. And as
that satisfied people, no further questions were
asked, and morals were saved.

So the Shah and his Astrologer were lodged
in the Royal palace, and looked for the stars
together when no visible stars were to be seen.
It was a concession of western prejudice to
eastern habit; and as that, too, resulted in a
treaty very conducive to trade, no earthly harm
came of it.

The Shah brilliantly attended many receptions, outshining all of them; and the wealth
and the power of the Nation was displayed
before him, but not the religion, and only a
very little of the morals. Many things he pro-
fessed to admire; by others he was manifestly
bored – they did not interest him. What did

interest, but still more puzzled him, was the position of women – the wedded and the un-wedded alike. He could not conceive how government or business could be conducted in a society where women not only mixed freely but showed their faces and their breasts.

Two Court functionaries accompanied him wherever he went – one to right and one to left – whose sole duty was to interpose with tactful and reverential gestures, and prevent the Son of Heaven from making preliminary advances upon the exposed charms of any court lady he was disposed to admire.

After he had been in the country for a week, he left off asking each member of the Royal Family whom he met how many wives he had. It had at last been borne in on him that they all had only one who could be publicly acknowledged. But he still continued to make interested inquiries concerning that one.

So, on meeting the Duke of Flamborough, he inquired as he had of others, 'You have a wife? Yes?'

The question was asked publicly before the Court; and the Court blushed. But the Duke, ever loyal to that one wise act of his youth, rose staunchly to the occasion. 'Yes, yes, sir! God damn it all, I have a wife. But I'm sensible like you, and I keep her in purdah, don't let her come out to be talked about. When she does go out, nobody knows anything about it.'

The Duke had answered handsomely but hastily, for never before in his life had such a question been put to him in the hearing of men; and unexpected questions and appearances always brought the Duke's mind to the charge. His words galloped in; he thought about them afterwards.

The embarrassed Court looked at Queen Augusta ; but she, as always, was equal to the occasion. She explained matters placidly; her domestic courage on occasion was tremendous. 'His Royal Highness, who is our cousin,' she said, 'married privately in his youth; the lady is his private wife, and does not appear publicly. We have allowed it to be. In this country, with our consent, it becomes permissible, and is quite in accordance with good morals.'

The interpreter translated. What he made of it can only be guessed. The Shah listened with opened eyes, full of expectancy and appetite.

'Eh? What?' he appeared to inquire. 'Is she then so much more beautiful than all the rest?'

Some such meaning to his words was passed on to the Duke.

'Why yes, sir; as beautiful as I want her to be; and a deal sight more beautiful than some who go about showing themselves.'

'I would like to see her,' said the Shah.

'And God damn it, sir, you shall!' said the Duke. And he did.

All this was through an interpreter. The Court had been tactfully drawn out of hearing by bands of myrmidons trained to etiquette from their birth; and, of course, when the visit took place, the actual fact had to be concealed under appearances which left nothing to be suspected.

The Shah went to dine at the Duke's official residence, with lines of troops and police and a great crowd in front to watch his arrival, and wait for his departure. And then, during the evening, when dinner was over, while in the large drawing-room – white, gold, and magenta – a brilliant and bowing company moved to and fro, up the paved garden with its urns and statues went the Shah and the Duke unbeknownst; through a back door and across a street and into a house more homely, and domestic, and comfortable than any the Shah had ever set foot in before, or dreamed even that any such thing could exist; and there, in the quiet boudoir of the lady whom society was not allowed to recognize, took coffee, and sweets, among the fragrance of freshly plucked roses, jasmine, and mignonette.

And the Shah said to her, 'Yes: you are beautiful. Your husband told me so; and this time it is true.'

To the Duke he said, 'I will buy her from you. How much?'

The Duke said, 'God damn it, sir! Not if you gave me your whole Kingdom.'

And the interpreter said, 'He says she is not worthy of your Heavenly acceptance. But if you will give him one half of your Kingdom he will consult the oracles and will let you know.'

And the Shah said, 'Meanwhile, I will consult my own Astrologer, and will ask him to comfort me.'

And he took from an attendant a diamond bracelet, more costly than any he had yet bestowed since leaving his own country, and clasped it upon the wrist of Mrs. Fitz-William. And Mrs. Fitz-William, curtsying low, drew her shawl over her head, over her beautiful face, covering it. An act of delicacy which the Shah had never seen done in that country before.

Oh, yes! The visit was a great success: but it remained a secret, till here, for the first time, it appears in print; and if the reader does not believe that it is true — the loss is his.

·

CHAPTER XIV

FAMILY LIFE

THE Duke's children – the children of Mr. Fitz-William, that is to say – took more after their father than their mother. They were not very intelligent, but they were well-behaved. Had they been more sharp and curious of intellect, the situation would have been more difficult. Even as it was, a sense of something mysterious about their father made its way into their minds at an early age. And since their parents chose not – while no one else in the house was permitted – to say anything, they resolved the mystery in their own way.

They decided that Papa was a burglar. It may seem a far-fetched explanation, since the absences of Mr. Fitz-William were more marked during the day than during the night. But his homecomings were generally late, and they seldom saw him except in the morning. Also they were impressed by the fact that he never went to church with them, nor was ever seen with them in public. Clearly, for some reason or another, he led a hidden life.

In those days illustrated weeklies were young, and illustrated newspapers non-existent. Photographs of celebrities had hardly yet begun to appear. Thus, on the publicity side of things, which to-day would have made concealment impossible, revelation of their father's exalted identity came late. Mrs. Fitz-William agreed with her husband that they had better not be told till the matter could be explained to them; but often she must have wondered whether discovery would abide the time thus fixed for it; for revealing it to one meant revealing it to all, and it might well be questioned whether the intelligence of the eldest could wait till the youngest was old enough to share the information.

It was a doubtful situation, and sometimes a difficult. Now and then the suppressed information became a live thing, like a snake's wriggle under a footmat; but the wriggle was not persistent, only premonitory; attention was successfully diverted, and the domestic life of the Fitz-Williamses went on with apocalypse still waiting round the corner.

Once, as the children turned over an illus-

trated magazine which their mother had forgotten previously to examine, she heard one of
them say sharply: 'That's like Papa!'

This must have given her a moment of un-
easiness; for if questioned it is doubtful whether
she would have lied about it. But she need not
have troubled; quick came the retort.

'No, it isn't! That isn't Papa's nose, nor his
eyes. And Papa's ever so much balder.'

It was all true; the illustrated magazine had
been too complimentary to give the secret away.
Nor did the children make any connection of
events when the Duke of Flamborough was
announced in the papers to have had an accident on the same day when Papa was brought
home with a badly bruised head, and a sprained
ankle, and a broken collar-bone; and both from
the same cause, a horse that had shied on meeting one of the new steam-engines.

But even this was not quite so unintelligent as
it may now appear: for the new steam-engines
had not yet been headed out of the streets into
tracks of their own, and the horses which did
not like them were numerous. The Duke's
accident hastened the passing of a by-law,
which dozens of previous accidents had not
been able to secure.

Nevertheless, Mr. Fitz-William's share in the

accident did have the effect of dismissing from the children's mind the idea that Papa was a burglar; for one of them chanced to overhear their mother telling their father that the Queen had sent to inquire after him. This, they felt sure, she would not have done, had he been a burglar. It was an exciting discovery. Viewing their father in the more favourable light thus cast on him, they decided that he must be the Queen's butler; and no longer so shy about the matter as they had been with their previous suspicions, they questioned Mamma how it was that the Queen had come to hear of his accident and why had she sent to inquire?

Mrs. Fitz-William replied quietly and without fluster, 'Because she knows him.' And when they asked further, 'Is he her butler?' she only laughed and said, 'There, run along and play!'

But when a little later, they discovered that they themselves had seen the Queen there in their own home, without knowing who she was, and that she was the lady they had been told to say 'Ma'am' to, and treat with such reverence, then their minds took a further run, and they got nearer the truth. 'I think,' said Henry, the eldest, 'that Papa is the Queen's chief executioner.'

After that, concealment became more difficult. Failing to get satisfaction from their parents, they began to ask the servants embarrassing questions, which the servants were not allowed to answer. And it may have been intelligent despair which caused their nurse, one fine day, to deflect their morning's walk in the direction of a small military parade which was just then crossing the Park.

This gave the situation away. 'That's Papa!' cried the children, pointing in wild excitement.

'How often have I told you not to point!' said nurse; and then, panic-stricken over what she had done, denying to them belief in the sight of their eyes, she hurried them home, assuring them all the way that it wasn't Papa but only somebody rather like him. It was useless, she was not believed.

To the credit of the Fitz-Williamses be it spoken, she was not dismissed for it. In some way or another this had to come; and now it had come dramatically, thrillingly, instantaneously to all three. The children were delighted, as any children would be who had previously thought their father a burglar, a butler, or an executioner, to discover that he was a soldier, and so great a soldier as to go riding ahead of the rest, wearing a cocked hat with plumes.

They broke the news to Mrs. Fitz-William

tumultuously; and she, taking it mildly and sensibly as she did everything, admitted that it was so. She had always intended to tell them some day, as wise mothers tell their inquiring children where babies come from, taking hens and their eggs for illustration. So now with the aid of fairy-tale and history she explained how princes had sometimes private families of their own, about which the world knew nothing; and that the private family itself must also pretend to know nothing; and she, making so little of it, reduced the wonder of its proportions to their minds; and when they next saw their father, they did not fall down and worship, but only giggled; and Henry said, 'We saw you!'

And John said, 'We saw you riding a horse.'

And Mary said, 'We saw you wearing a cocked hat!'

And Mr. Fitz-William, whom his wife had previously prepared for the situation, said, 'Well, and what if you did? Have you never seen a man and a horse, and a cocked hat before? You'll find them in the Park like mushrooms any day. Now if you'd met me turned into a crocodile, it would have been something to talk about.'

'No, it wouldn't,' said Mary, 'I should have run away.'

'I shouldn't,' said Henry, 'I should have gone and got a big stick, and killed you!'

John said, 'No, you wouldn't! He'd have killed *you*.'

Mrs. Fitz-William said, 'Even if he were a crocodile, I don't think he'd be dangerous.'

It was a certificate of character – though, in a certain direction, it may have stood for defects. But in that direction the Fitz-William household was not concerned.

Into this quiet pool of domesticity the projectile had been thrown, but had not disturbed it; the ripples of discovery spread quietly over its surface – touched shore, subsided, were absorbed, became insignificant. The knowledge that their father was a member of the Royal Family and the Commander-in-Chief of an Army, should surely have made him a formidable and romantic figure in the eyes of his children; but it did not.

'It's funny,' said Mary, aged seven.

Family life had triumphed: the new knowledge had done no harm to anyone.

But now that they were aware, it did add interest; for the next time Queen Augusta came to call they knew who she was; and behaved so appallingly well that she noticed the difference. Deducing from this that they now knew who

they were – that is to say, who their father was
– 'Have you been telling them, Fanny?' she
asked disapprovingly, when she and Mrs. Fitz-
William were once more alone.

'Practically they found out for themselves.'

'How very awkward for you and poor
William,' said Augusta.

Mrs. Fitz-William smiled. 'They haven't
made it awkward for us,' she said. ' They don't
seem to think much about it.'

'Oh?' Augusta was not quite pleased. 'I
should have thought that it made a great
difference.'

'Originally of course, it did,' replied Mrs.
Fitz-William; 'but they have been brought up
to the difference; and having never had other
expectations are now accustomed to it.'

Queen Augusta did not quite know what to
say, she had decided that the relationship was
moral, otherwise she would not be there; but
it did not please her that they were not a little
ashamed of it. And telling it to the children –
that certainly should have been awkward.
Fanny was very beautiful and sweet; but she a
little too strong-minded. In that respect, however, William made up for her. And yet on that
one point – his private marriage – he was
strong-minded also: he observed the conven-

tions about it, as his position required, but he was not ashamed of it.

Mrs. Fitz-William was wrong, however, about the impression it had made on the children. It interested and engaged their thoughts much more than she knew. And when they were admitted to their father's dressing-room to see him shave in the morning – a family habit which association had endeared to them, – Mary would say to herself as she watched Mr. Fitz-William plying the razor – 'Now he is shaving the Duke of Flamborough.'

CHAPTER XV

THE COLLECTIONS OF
ROYALTY

IT is not necessary for Royalty to be as much
interested in things intellectual and artistic, as
in things material. Mind is always a minority
interest, except when it turns to finance, war, or
politics; and the Crown, to keep its public,
must let its tastes go with the majority.

The tastes and pursuits of Royalty are bound
therefore to be popular, and allow nothing but
what the bulk of the public approves to attract
its exalted attention. For if Royalty looks at a
picture in public, the picture sells; and if
Royalty lets its liking for a certain author to be
known, the author runs into editions; yet never
in its long life has it been known to encourage a
neglected author, destined after his death to
become famous. Royal minds have seldom the
gift of prophecy, or even of cultured discern-
ment; between them and the great ones of

literature there is sometimes a bowing acquaintance, but no intimacy; and for artists,
they prefer those who paint dogs aping the
sentiments of humanity, or toy battle-pieces
which make cavalry charges look like greased
lightning, and squares of infantry like the rock
whence heroes are hewn, and portraits like
toilet-soap advertisements. On such artists as
these minor honours are conferred when they
have achieved popularity, but never on those
others of more disputed genius who have missed
it. Which only goes to prove what a very representative institution monarchy still is.

Queen Augusta was quite frank about the
matter: it was not consistent with her dignity,
she said, to have conversation conducted in her
presence by persons of superior intellect on
subjects in which she could not take the lead.
And on the one and only occasion when she met
Gargoyle, that great but grumpy philosopher,
she found safety in receptive silence, allowing
conversation to become the monologue to
which habit had accustomed him. It happened
also that he chose his subject well; Augusta
having made kind inquiries about his dead wife,
he discoursed on death and the burial customs
of ancient races, the savage and the civilized;
and Augusta was quite interested, having burial

customs of her own awaiting her demise, with an embalmer in close attendance wherever she went, who occupied the leisure her longevity imposed on him in the stuffing of rare birds.

But though the members of the Royal Family did not strain themselves to intellectual heights in the direction of art and literature, they had a conscientious wish to encourage culture, and even to take a mild share in it. And it had been discovered for them that the easiest way to do this was to become collectors.

Collecting is not difficult when the subject is well-chosen. If it has not become so great a rarity as to have flooded the market with spurios, it does not require expert knowledge – only patience, plodding perseverance, and a certain expenditure of time and money. Hit on a subject that no one else has thought of, and your collection may become unrivalled. It must not be pictures or postage stamps, or the folios of Shakespeare, for over these America will beat even Royalty; and the collector's path is dogged by forgeries. But a forged 'bus ticket is unknown; you can therefore, without strain of intellect or fear of being cheated, collect 'bus tickets. But you can never make your collection even approximately complete; and that, from the collector's point of view, is a drawback. A collection, to be notable, must have before it an attainable measure of completeness. And perhaps that is why no member of the Royal Family collected 'bus tickets. For them, indeed, it would be peculiarly difficult, since they never used one. But an examination of what they did collect – based perhaps on that consideration of completeness combined with intellectual ease – may be interesting to the psychologist.

H.R.H. the Duke of Toller collected fleas – dead ones. Out of two hundred and fifty-three known varieties he had managed to secure a hundred and seventy-eight; but this not being by personal research and capture, it lacked something of individual interest, and could not even be classed as 'small game hunting.'

H.R.H. Prince Lewis, on entering the Army as a cadet, collected drumsticks. But though a pair for every regiment of every Army which employed drumsticks would make the collection complete from a military point of view, there still remained the drumsticks of Punch and Judy, and also of the savage races. Completion was going to be difficult.

H.R.H. Princess Amelia collected photographs of Royalties with large moustaches: of these the King of Italy had the largest which were genuine throughout, though it was a difficult point to decide where moustache ended and whisker began.

A Prince of the House of Austria had a pair with longer ends; but these being reputed to have a join in them under the wax, she regarded as spurious. It was a stimulating collection, and the Princess had additional pleasure in getting them autographed.

H.R.H. Princess Sophia collected crests; five hundred crests of Royalty, and nineteen thousand of the nobility of Europe were the sum total of her collection. It was practically complete.

From these we pass to the most interesting collection of all.

The Duke of Flamborough collected buttons. Metal buttons, bone buttons, jet buttons, cloth buttons, leather buttons, braid buttons, buttons of gold, silver and ivory, buttons of inlay, buttons of mosaic, perforated buttons, round buttons, square buttons, boot-buttons, tail-coat buttons, foil-buttons, buttons from the hats of Chinese Mandarins, buttons from the breeches worn by Napoleon at Waterloo, buttons from the gloves worn by Queen Augusta at her Coronation, a button that had saved a King's life, a button (of silver) employed as a bullet for shooting a wizard; but above all, and more

numerous than all in their ordered variety, the
regimental buttons of all the Armies of Europe,
from the days when regiments began to wear
buttons in place of the straps and laces they had
worn previously.

And this, indeed, was the reason why he had
begun collecting them. For in the Duke's
annual addresses to the Army a passion for
buttons became manifest, and the polishing of
buttons made a trinitarian unity with the
rigidity of the salute, and the mechanical per-
fection of drill. Given these, as demonstrated
on parade, and he had the Army of his
ideal.

But though regimental buttons were the
raison d'être of the collection, its most striking
exhibit was a specimen culled from the market-
place. Standing central in the small museum,
which he kept not in his official but in his
private residence – was a stuffed effigy, dressed
in corduroys, completely covered by pearl buttons. It was a costume which had once belonged to the King of the Costers. How the
Duke came by it, and through what adventures
hung on to it, is now to be told.

It was a late acquisition. The Duke had been
collecting buttons for many years when he set
eyes on these. And just as an Eastern Sheikh is

prepared to give up heart and soul and conscience for possession, at sight of some Arab
mare, so the Duke, sighting these for the first
time, was prepared to go great lengths for the
possession of them.

He did not at first conceive that there would
be any difficulty. He had encountered them at
the parade of dray-horses held annually in one
of the public parks; when, after the horses, had
come costers and their mokes. And driving
these, men not with the stature of angels – for
the breed was small – but with glistering white
apparel like gates of pearl, more beautiful to
look upon than the state robes of an Eastern
potentate. And among these lilies of the slums
went one – the King of them – wearing from
top to toe (for his cap was peaked and his boots
were tipped with them) a computed total of
seven thousand four hundred pearl buttons of
various shapes and sizes, sewn into a wondrous
galaxy of curves, bands, and patterns, with
hardly a space between, save where, when
sitting down, it did not show.

The Duke had graced the occasion with his
presence for the encouragement of horse-breeding; but like Romeo who, going to the ball
hungry for Rosaline, stayed to sup on Juliet,
so he, when this apparition of pearliness broke

into view, forsook his simulated love of horse-flesh and thought only of buttons.

Lust of possession entered into him, without however making too great a disturbance, for he was confident that the figure he was willing to name would be sufficient. And so, when the King of the Costers had passed the point of salute, he sent one of his gentlemen after him to make a tentative offer, and to report.

The gentleman came back with word that the suit was not for sale; but he had taken the fellow's name and address. Fifty pounds had been offered him, and though unwilling, the owner was greatly impressed with the sense of his importance.

The Duke, always a man for immediate action when roused, sent his gentleman again to adumbrate a yet higher price, and to make, circumspectly, an appointment for the man to be more personally interviewed.

And so that same evening, bringing the clothes with him, he came to the house of a Mr. Williams (the name quite ordinary) and was seen by Mr. Williams himself.

The man, with a self-possession which did credit to his class, refrained from recognizing him. For, be it remembered, he had that day passed the saluting-point, where the Duke looking his ordinary self had worn mufti; also in his past youth the man had been a unit in the militia, and at his annual training had taken part in manœuvres over which the Duke had presided. But what the man must have thought of this surreptitious bargaining of Royalty under an assumed name can only be gathered from what happened afterwards.

Before going to bed that night the Duke recorded the matter in his diary; the bargain was struck, and the pearlies changed hands price one hundred pounds. The Duke wrote a cheque for the amount on his domestic bankers – his signature the usual one.

That should have concluded the matter, but did not. Next day the man came again, and insisted obstreperously, in spite of secretarial intervention, on another interview. He had come from domestic storm. He had calculated, he said, the cost of his seven thousand odd pearlies, the value of the design and the rarity of it, with something extra thrown in for the association and sentiment of years; and he had reckoned, out of this, to buy himself a new suit and seven or eight thousand new buttons, so that his kingship should not pass to another. But his wife, he found, objected to restoring him his kingdom by so large a labour of love as this demanded of her, unless she also were paid for it. And the long and the short of it was that he and she wanted between them another hundred pounds.

When the Duke heard that, he told his secretary to kick the fellow out; and the secretary, in a quiet manner of speaking, did so; saw the angry little man to the doorstep, and shut the door on his protestations. A policeman, passing on his beat, superintended his further removal. And that again should have concluded the matter, but did not.

Two nights later the Duke was awakened by a noise, and going forth from his chamber adequately armed to meet burglars, encountered one with a face he knew carrying under his arm the suit of pearlies.

Then ensued, amid a full flow of expletives, claim and counter-claim, asseveration and denial; and neither giving way to the other, the Duke made threat presently to call in the police; whereat the man, laying down the pearlies, and the uncashed cheque for a demonstration of confident mastery of the situation, said reasoningly and sweetly, 'But you can't do it, Governor, you know you can't!'

And as the Duke, obtuse of intellect, seemed *not* to know it, he proceeded to explain why;

214

and if we had the material for giving it in the man's own words the exposition would be a more entertaining one. For now the Duke heard that he had been recognized; and here he was, in a house where he was not supposed to be, calling himself Mr. Williams, which was one name, and signing a cheque in another, and neither of them his right name; and if he gave this man in charge to the police, and if the man's lawyer subpœnaed him as a witness for the defence, where would he be – and what would he say about it? Would it anyway be worth the extra hundred pounds which was all that a poor man, speaking in his poor wife's interests, was demanding?

At this point a sound came, from the open door of the bedroom; the Duke turned to attend to it. 'It's all very well for you to laugh, my dear!' he said.

'Asking the lady's pardon,' said the man, seizing the domestic situation, 'now doesn't she agree that what I says is reasonable?'

Apparently she did. The Duke amended the cheque; and the pearlies remained in his possession, going at his death to the Municipal Museum by bequest – the only item in his vast collection of buttons worth the money it had cost him, in the delight it was to give to the eyes of future generations when Coster Kings had become an extinct species, and their apparel of such a rarity as to be practically unobtainable.

CHAPTER XVI

DECLINING YEARS

As the Duke advanced in years, his relations with Queen Augusta, which had always been correct since that one episode into which the counsel of the Uncles had betrayed him, became more intimate and cordial. The Uncles were now all dead, so were others nearer and dearer, in whom the Queen had placed both confidence and affection; favourite ministers had gone, giving place to others who were no favourites. Into religion, society and politics new ideas were entering, with which she had little sympathy; also the survivors of her large family were now all grown-up, and some of her sons were troublesome.

Augusta was one who put more faith in the yesterdays of life than in its to-morrows, and mistrusting youth to the verge of disapproval, gave increasing confidence, as they aged, to those whose opinions were similar to her own.

And in opinion, though not in character, she and the Duke were birds of a feather. They had a common dislike for change, and a common suspicion of the characters of those who insisted that change was necessary. For which reason, in relation to politics, the life of Queen Augusta had been a life of growing suspicion; for in politics things seemed never to rest; the political system of alternate governments being in itself subversive of order and stability, with so much time spent by each in turn, in undoing the mischief of its predecessor, and then, when that was done, preparing the ground for its own departure by a series of blunders which, even in downfall, it would never own to.

But in the Army, as commanded by the Duke, things were far otherwise; there the changes were few and unimportant, and of most of them, when consulted beforehand, the Queen was able to approve. Having a near relative at the head made things so much easier, for here she was able to send letters direct, without the consultation of ministers, and everything that she wrote received, if not agreement, attention. Thus, when war had again disturbed the peace of the Nation, and had begun badly for reasons which neither she nor the Duke could penetrate, the day following a review of troops called up for service she wrote to him as follows:

'In the midst of so much that is tragic and distressing – and who to blame for it I'm sure I don't know; but that I am sure you will make it your duty to find out and *correct*, when all is over – I forgot a trifle, but still which I think ought not to be left any longer unattended to. It is the *moustaches* as regards the *men and officers serving* (I don't mean any of the old Generals, etc., to whom one would not wish to seem personal); but for those actually upon service it should no longer be *optional* but *ordered* to be worn. The effect in the ranks is altogether bad, and most noticeable when you see some with and some without them. I think this should now be done without delay, as while on active service the discipline should be stricter.'

In this same war a Prince, in retirement from the service of his own country, had volunteered in order to get military experience; and instead, escaping from the safe tutelage which had been arranged for him, had managed to get killed. For this, of course, the Duke was in no way responsible; but somebody was, and the Queen wrote her mind on the matter, which – as it indicates the position Royalty expects to take in modern warfare – is worth quoting:

'How it could have happened that a *Prince* should be allowed to get into such a dangerous position is quite inexplicable, and most negligible of somebody, which ought certainly to be found out, and steps taken. Surely *He* was, by the original arrangement, *never* to have left the General. Such a thing ought *not* to have been allowed, and I *greatly fear* that we shall be blamed for it. Who could have done such a thing is to me quite unimaginable.'

To all such plaints as these the Duke was sympathetic, and said the right thing; and Augusta, reading his kind answers, felt that her confidence had been rightly placed. He always listened to her, and was never impatient; so different from some of her ministers, one of whom, for that reason, she had had to dismiss.

While this same war was going on abroad, and he directing it from at home, so far as stay-at-home direction was possible, the Duke was not immune from having to meet situations which were a trial to nerves that had once faced the ordeal of battle. Though every inch a warrior, he had a sensitive nature, as the following quotation from the diary shows:

'Going in state to the opening of the new Military Museum, two postilions of the second carriage-and-four fell in the street, their horses frightened by the cheering. Luckily no one was hurt, which, to look at, was certainly a miracle. I never saw anything more horrid to behold; so much so that we had to transfer ourselves to another carriage – very undignified and embarrassing, and a lot of shifting to be done with people all looking on. We saw them getting up again all right as we passed, nobody hurt, nor the horses. But this sort of thing ought never to happen. The populace behaved quite well considering how very far they might have been from knowing better.'

This happened in the Duke's sixty-third year, and to a man of his age and sense of ceremonial importance, was certainly a very trying ordeal to go through.

A year later, when the war was over, criticism of the Army's efficiency began to make itself heard in the Press, and from then on there continued to be rumblings of discontent, inside and outside of Parliament, for the next thirteen or fourteen years, till the great change was finally brought about which ended the Duke's career.

The trouble began with a proposal (based on recent experience in the field) for the conversion of certain regiments from cavalry into mounted infantry, accompanied by the abolition of swords. The Duke, believing in tradition as the father of efficiency, fought against both changes, but fought in vain: the thing was done over his head by Act of Parliament. The diary records his failure to make wiser counsels prevail – his first experience of a diminution of influence which thereafter he was increasingly to realize:

'This is a sad day for me, and one which I had hoped to be spared. It has been decided to make great changes in the Army, in spite of my earnest remonstrances; but I have not succeeded in preventing anything – a result I greatly deplore. Alas that I shall not live to see them realize their mistake. Life is a great mystery; and I feel that my days are numbered.'

Elsewhere, before a Ministerial Board set up by Government to investigate and make recommendations for the reorganization of the Army, he gave a more reasoned statement of his objections. In his evidence before it, he thus expressed himself:

'What the Army wants is *rest* from constant surprises. I am afraid your Board undervalues tradition, and does not believe in sentiment. I do so, and have done all my life, especially in military matters. I am prepared to do all I can to induce the present Yeomanry Regiments to attend more to their carbines than their swords, and substitute target-practice for sword-exercise; but to *deprive* them of their swords, the distinguishing feature of cavalry from the beginning of history, and make mounted infantry of them – which is a contradiction in words – would I consider completely destroy the force and take all the heart out of them.'

This view he reported to Queen Augusta, and she entirely agreed with him. 'The Board has been set up,' she told him in reply, 'in complete opposition to my wishes and opinions; and had Lord Benzaline been still in office would never have happened. It is sad to think what a lot of *wicked* things are being done, and *we* powerless to prevent them.'

And just at this very time the desirable Lord Benzaline dies, in dignified retirement from office, full of years and honour.

On the day after this event the Duke writes:

'My sixty-third birthday. How old I am! I feel that I am getting much sadder; but am I wiser? It is very difficult to think so, when one has so many fools to contend against, whom one is unable to prevent. Heard yesterday of the death of Lord Benzaline: a dreadful blow to all right-thinking people, of whom, alas! there are not enough in the country to go round so as to form a majority.'

Shortly after, the Duke comes into conflict with one of the leading organs of public opinion which has started a series of articles on Army Reform written – its readers are informed – 'under the auspices of the highest military authority.' To this the Duke made public reference at the annual Civic Banquet, when having to respond to the toast of the Army.

'I was not till now aware,' he said, 'that "the highest military authority" could mean any but one thing; and I only can say, in reference to the published views to which I am referring, that I have the very best reason to believe that "the highest military authority" – which up to this moment I believed I was – is not me but some other person who chooses for reasons best known to himself to remain nameless, and whose opinions, I hope I may be allowed to say, I do not share.'

This disavowal, though emphatic, did not, however, give the desired quietus to the articles in question. As they went on they got worse, creating, as the Duke presently complained, 'a dangerously uninformed state of public opinion, subversive of all the traditions on which the Army prides itself.'

Presently out into the open came the stark proposal, which had so long been germinating in the minds of the Duke's critics and opponents, for the abolition of the post of Commander-in-Chief. It found voice in Parliament, and was respectfully listened to. 'A most deplorable recommendation,' was the Duke's comment when he heard of it. From Queen Augusta he received the welcome assurance that she was 'fully determined to retain the position *unimpaired.*'

Unfortunately, it was impaired already. Where for so many years his decisions had been final, the Duke was no longer to have the last word. Retaining his command under its old title, he is forced, in the thirtieth year of his appointment, to enter into relations (which sometimes become subordinate) with the Minister for War; and when they think differently, it is the Minister's will that prevails.

'I never thought,' he writes in his diary, 'that such a thing would be done without my consent, and the Queen also against it. I must own that I am disgusted with this, to my mind, most un-justifiable proceeding of placing the civilian point of view over the trained military one. Of this I am quite sure – it did not come from the Army, but from the minds of those radical politicians who are bent on destroying it.'

Under these sad circumstances he receives, on his sixty-fifth birthday, a kind letter from Queen Augusta which cheers him:

'MY DEAR WILLIAM, –

'Your birthday, coming as it *always* does, the day after that of my dear faithful servant, Polter – *a red letter day* in my calendar, and that I make a point of remembering, he always knowing that I shall *never* forget him – I am reminded as I do now, and write to wish you *many many* happy returns of the day which increasing age makes so sad and full of memories for both of us. This time I gave him a biscuit-box to have at his bedside, which I hope is not too much con-sidering all the *devoted* service he has given to me and my family during the last thirty years. To you, dear Cousin, I am sending a clinical thermometer which is one of the *newest* and most *useful* medical inventions I know. I use it myself constantly, so I hope you, too, will find the benefit of it, as a *warning*, if you should ever feel you are going to be ill.

'I trust also that it will help you to bear the great responsibility and *risks* of looking after my dear Army *in all weathers*, which you do with so much devotion and knowledge of its requirements. *And*, in spite of what *others* may say, you shall continue to do so, so long as *I* have *any* voice in the matter.

'I wanted to let you *know* what was in my *mind*: and this seemed a suitable occasion, though not, I hope, the last *for many years*.

'Believe me, my dear William,
   'Your very affectionate Cousin,
                              'AUGUSTA.'

The rift – or was it rather to be called the interference? – had begun more than ten years earlier, with the advent of a Minister who, having a definite mind of his own, was – when either came in the way – no respecter of tradition or of Royalty. And having conceived a vision of what the military machine should

227

look like and act like, different from the Duke's
vision so full of beautiful yesterdays in which
morrows had no place – he, believing that
Armies like other things must move with the
times, had begun trying to get his way, first
over quite small things for an experiment, just
as you tap at crumbling mortar before heaving
out the stones of an old wall. And over the quite
small things the Duke had withstood him valiantly and persistently, as though instinct told
him that these were, indeed, the mortar which
held his old edifice of an Army together.

It had begun over buttons, which were the
Duke's strong point; intellectually the Duke's
mind was composed entirely of buttons and
button-holes; and where these fitted and joined,
they gave him a mental equipment closed to
innovations. Not for nothing was the Duke a
collector of buttons; on these he justly felt himself to be an expert and an authority; and when
a new type of button for the Army was set before
his eyes, though as a collector he might have
welcomed, as an Army commander he rejected
it. The question posed was the military effect of
the substitution of round-headed buttons for flat
ones, and of hard bullet-proof metal for soft.
The Duke was for the flat button. A button, he
said, from which the bullet glanced off might

cause more casualties in the ranks than one
which merely stopped its impetus before allow-
it to sink into the body it was aimed at. He had
it tried on dummies for a demonstration; but the
bullets so seldom hit a button of either kind,
that the demonstration proved inconclusive.

The argument that the new type would be
easier to button, he met by saying that the
making of things easier was not conducive to
discipline; further, he objected that what would
button more easily would also unbutton more
easily, and an army unbuttoned would be as
ineffective as an army fighting with arms
reversed.

Nevertheless, in spite of his resistance, the
new button was introduced, and within three
years the Army had settled down into preferring
it to the old one. It took that time, for Armies
are by nature conservative; and the Duke in his
resistance to change had its instincts with him –
up to the point when practice caused instincts
to modify.

In the battle of the buttons, which was his
first defeat, the Duke limited himself to argument and strong language, of which he had a
remarkable flow undiminished by age; but over
the altered pattern of the forage-cap, which
came next, and the position this was to occupy

on the head of its wearer, he felt the matter so deeply that he took to his bed for a fortnight, with loss of voice and other distressing symptoms; and during the whole of that time was unable to append his signature to any document. Commissions in the Army were held up by it; and a few regiments and their horses had to be put on short rations pending the authorization of fresh supplies. It was a demonstration of what being a Commander-in-Chief in those days meant; and though intended to give the civilian Minister an object-lesson in co-ordination and unity of command, he failed to profit by it in the direction intended.

The altered pattern of the bayonet had come earlier; but though he had a sentimental preference for bayonet wounds to be flat and sword-like rather than triangular, the Duke minded that much less than other things which he had felt less able to resist. The introduction of the gatling-gun (imposed by its success elsewhere) had sent a shock to the foundation of all his sentiments and traditions. For this he felt to be the thin edge of socialism: indiscriminate mechanical slaughter, operated by the mere turning of a wheel, without any picked marksmanship required in its manipulation, reduced – he felt – the individual and human element of soldiering to a minimum. 'They'll go doing it with their eyes shut,' he said. And if that became normal, how were they going to 'see red' he wanted to know; and without 'seeing red' how did they think battles were going to be won?

He himself during his brief period of active service had on several occasions, and once especially, seen very red indeed. He knew, therefore, the value of it, and was not going to have it eliminated from the Army without a struggle. But it was the Duke's sad fate to be living through a transitional period when, in things military, sentiment was giving place to science.

Sentimentally there never was a better Army than that which the Duke commanded and had in his own way perfected. It was popular, and beautiful to look upon, and it cost more per head than any other army in the world. On a small scale it was a pattern of what an Army, looked at merely as a pattern and a receptacle for ancient traditions, was expected to be. But on the field of battle the pattern went sadly to pieces; and though, when that happened, tradition held its ground nobly and died unflinchingly for the incompetence of its commanders, the Country did not like to have even as few as three hundred lives extinguished by even as many as five thousand savages. A defeat was a defeat however glorious; and since defeats had been practically eliminated from its textbooks of history, the Country felt that tradition was not being truly maintained under the Duke's management; and gradually, very gradually, the demand gathered volume that something should be done differently in the carrying on of the military traditions of the past.

And there, in the way, stood the Duke, monumental, immovable, of Royal blood, a near relative to the Crown and now nearly seventy years of age. How, with sufficient respect, was a long-suffering nation to ask him to get out of the way?

It took six more years respectfully to do it, years of uncomfortable waiting, while the Army continued unprogressively to mark time. It was during this period that the Duke did his Country that great act of service which has never been recorded, imposing upon the Government a peace-policy (which he himself highly disapproved of), by the extreme inefficiency for field service of the Army under his command. It was lucky that the civilian Minister found this out before the Government had finally committed itself. The Duke himself would never have done so.

232

And yet had the Government gone to war, and had the inevitable catastrophe followed, the Duke, in all probability, would still have got his statue; so great is the glamour of Royalty in the heart of a conservative-minded people.

CHAPTER XVII

'OBITER DICTA'

IN the course of his public career the Duke was obliged to make a great many speeches. During the earlier part of it, they were made for him; but after becoming Head of the Army he made his own, which, before appearing in the Press, were extensively edited – not only for grammatical but for other reasons as well.

Even in the official records of the House of Peers, which are supposed to be verbatim, discreet alterations had to be made. A committee of the Cabinet would anxiously sit over them and decide how much might safely be left; and since the original records were carefully destroyed, it is impossible to say how far this ministerial editing went.

The public occasion on which the Duke best liked speaking, was the annual Civic Banquet when, having dined well, he spoke, as the official Head of the Army, to the most distinguished gathering of all the talents for which occasion could be found. There, speaking in the hearing of lords, judges, ladies, archbishops, financiers, speculators, owners of race-horses, men of business, and representatives of all departments of the public service, he let himself go, and in a genial rambling sort of way 'saw red' for the Nation. Then, of whatever came uppermost in his mind, he spoke; and the élite of society sat and listened to him – respectfully.

As a sample of his style of oratory, we give here the published version – probably less edited than usual – of his remarks about scare in war-time ('scare,' in his sense of it, meaning criticism of the Army) made while a small war was still going on.

'The fact is,' said the Duke, 'and this is the long and short of it – in times of excitement the only thing for every one to do, from the highest to the lowest, is to do his duty in that station of life to which it has pleased God to call him; and to leave those in the other stations alone to do theirs. But I venture to say, looking at the facts which just now I consider deplorable, that if all the gossip which goes round in times of excitement goes back to the base, or gets into the papers, or anywhere else, then every sort of

statement is put forward as true which is not
true, and the excitement becomes positively
dangerous, and is bad in its results on discipline
and efficiency, and may even become disastrous,
which, if people would hold their tongues, it
wouldn't have.'

Thus he marshalled his case for a voluntary
Press-censorship in war-time, appealing to
editors not to publish any such statements unless convinced they were based on truth and
justice, and not to allow sensational articles to
appear 'for no better purpose than the mere
object of having them sold in the streets by a
lot of little boys late at night when they ought
to be in bed.'

And having thus mothered his Army in the
field with all his power, and protected it from
crude blasts of criticism, he would see in the
head-lines of his paper the next day: 'Remarkable speech by the Duke,' 'Startling Home
Truths,' 'Scare-mongers scarified,' and then
would read how he had made 'a stirring and
patriotic speech full of wisdom and common
sense, delivered with that independence of
judgment and soldierly directness of expression
which we are accustomed to look for,' etc., etc.
And this, in the leading organ of the day: was
it any wonder with such backing that the Duke

believed himself to be the right man in the right place, and with public opinion behind him?

This particular war, we learn in the diary, forced the Duke to give up his game-shooting for the year. He seems to have made the sacrifice with more difficulty than he would have done in early youth; custom had bred a liking. There are three entries in the diary of regret over cancelled engagements.

In his Art Banquet speeches the Duke was less happy. He knew that he was there to be complimentary over things he did not much care about. All he could do was to go round and pick out the portraits in uniform, and the battle-pieces, and with these for evidence give it as his opinion that art was still flourishing, and could, he ventured to say, compare favourably with the art of any other country or any other age.

But having to speak on the same occasion for many years in succession, even to himself such remarks became threadbare from repetition, and he felt forced to provide variety; and then, though truly speaking from his heart, he would get out of his depth and say things which would have been right twenty years before, but were not so right when he said them – since Art and

237

the opinions that formed round it moved forward faster than the army and the mind which commanded it.

So when he spoke of Wagner as the main cause of the growing estrangement between two nations once friendly and allied, there was embarrassment in his audience; for Wagner was just then 'the thing.' And when he said that, with all respect to the fine spirit and independence shown by American industry, we did not need Americans to teach us how to paint portraits in a fog, having fogs enough of our own, there was yet more embarrassment, for though the foggy American he referred to was not among his audience, another very distinguished American was; and he, whose portraits more resembled the sound of a brass trumpet, was beginning to be the vogue and to have imitators.

And the Duke was dimly aware that on these occasions he was not a success; he was ill at ease with his surroundings and was glad when it was all over.

At religious gatherings he did better; for the Church, which claimed to be a kind of Army and called itself 'militant,' had, like his own, a tendency to mark time and to regard proposed changes with disapproval. He was also a loyal supporter of state-established religion and no

238

other. Speaking on one occasion to a gathering
of Army chaplains he said: 'I do not see why
anybody who goes into the Army should wish to
belong to anything but the established religion.
When you go into the Army you give your
conscience to the State, and the State looks
after it for you, and provides Chaplains for the
purpose. A soldier has got to believe in God
somehow, or he couldn't believe in anything –
couldn't do his job either. You have to believe
in God when it's your duty to go out and kill
your fellow-creatures; it's your only excuse for
doing it. It's harder sometimes to believe in
your Commanding Officer, when he gives you
an order that looks damned silly, and may be a
mistake. And established religion is the best
training for believing what you've got to believe,
and not trouble your head too much about it,
which is what makes a good soldier. It's the
religion that has done most for the country; and
if it's good enough for me is good enough for
those who are under me. Its foreign missions
have helped to give us our colonies, at much
less trouble and expense and loss of life than
we should have got them otherwise. And the
mortality among missionaries, considering
cannibals and all that sort of thing, has been
remarkably small and promising, the Army

having backed them up. Therefore I consider, and I say, that the Established Church has a right to be the Church of the Army. Anyway we can prevent the other denominations from becoming officers.'

He spoke, and the chaplains respectfully applauded. What he said about other denominations was actually true. Until the Duke laid down his baton, there was no such thing as a Free-Church commissioned officer to be found; partly, no doubt, because in his day no Free Churchman was considered a gentleman; and an officer had to be not only a gentleman himself but the son of a gentleman.

It is an interesting fact that this fine social distinction was largely broken down by the growing wealth and importance of the brewing-trade. A millionaire brewer sent one of his younger sons into the army; and though it was against all rules, he was so large a contributor to the funds of his party that the War Office had to be instructed to make an exception in his son's favour. It was the beginning of the end.

The Duke's view of religion was, as the above remarks will have shown, a very simple one: patriotism came first. He was pious, but national in his Christianity: the national translation of the Bible superseded the original

Hebrew in authenticity and spiritual authority.
He did not profess to be a theologian; but when,
apropos of a running down of the Jews, some one
remarked in his hearing that Christ Himself was
one, he considered the reminder slightly blas-
phemous, and countered it by the retort: 'Only
on His mother's side'; a statement so crushing
in its theological accuracy as to leave nothing
more to be said.

He had these inspirations now and again, and
was fond of drawing scriptural parallels to the
wonders of modern invention, but always in
favour of the former as the more marvellous.
Had he lived into the coming age of submarines
he would have cited Jonah's whale, as he did
Balaam's Ass when a clown's donkey was making a fortune for its master at the Courts of
Europe. And the fact that Ezekiel had foreseen
flying-machines, and had accurately described
them, would presumably have prejudiced him in
their favour, as an authorized addition to the
inventions of war.

He did not care much for the theatre, though
sometimes he had to go, when the performance
was a 'command' one. The opera he detested
as three plagues rolled into one; and how he
regarded Wagner has already been told.

Of his meeting with the rulers of foreign

states, either visiting or visited, his diary records a fine shade of difference which remains invariable. They please him under one of two heads. The Kings he meets are 'gracious' in their demeanour towards him, Presidents of Republics are 'modest.' On those terms, and those only, he approves of them; for always in his eyes a nation which had become a Republic was as one who, in marriage, has made a misalliance – publicly.

Science troubled him: its complexities carried him entirely out of his depth; and having nothing safe to say about it, he avoided it so far as public recognition was concerned. In the army, as we know, he fought it to the death.

'Also I don't like astronomy,' he once said. 'It unsettles people; and it isn't practical. You don't get any nearer to a star by pretending to know what it's made of. You can study it till your brain splits: what's the good? If God had intended us to know anything about stars, He'd have told us – in the Bible.'

'But is knowledge, Sir,' some one objected, ' – permissible knowledge – limited to what is found in the Scriptures?'

'Knowledge of the things that don't concern us,' said the Duke, '*is* limited to the Scriptures, and by the Scriptures. And if the world has

lasted longer than six thousand years, and all
that – as they are trying to make out now –
then all I say is that it's no better than it should
be, but a deal worse. If it has been six thousand
years, there has been some improvement to
show for it: but if it has already been six hundred thousand, we are never going to get
anywhere.'

When, in the Duke's view of the world, it may
be asked, 'had it begun to improve?' Probably
he would have said at the Reformation, when
sea-power came to the assistance of religion, and
Protestant got the better of Catholic. Till then,
all religion was superstition, the Duke was once
heard to say. 'Now the danger's the other way:
we aren't superstitious enough – and that's all
about it! You've got to be superstitious about
some things – things you can't otherwise be sure
of – or where are you?'

Out of the mouths of babes! Almost at that
very time a poet whom the Duke had never read
– hadn't even heard of – had written a poem
called 'Bishop Blougram's Apology,' saying
almost the same thing.

Careless readers may think that the Duke's
objections to change, so many of which have
now been given, were unreasonable. That is a
mistake; he always had a reason, a definite one,

and could give it. And more often than not, from his point of view, it was a true reason. When, for instance, abolition of the purchase system for Commissions in the Army was proposed, the Duke was strongly against it, and gave his reasons. From the Duke's point of view they were unanswerable.

'So long as you sell Commissions,' he said, 'you know who you are selling them to. But if once you begin letting them in by examination, you don't know what you may be getting. You can keep a radical out by refusing to accept his money; but you can't keep him out by refusing to accept his brains – if the silly ass has got any – once you make examination the test. If you are going to lead your Army on book-knowledge and brains, then the Army is not going to stand on its feet any more, but on its head, and I'm out of it.'

The remark was prophetic, as regards himself; yet though abolition took place the very next year, his own retirement did not follow for twenty.

But the most accurate specimen we have of the Duke's power of argument, and marshalling of facts, is in the set speech, followed by debate, which was taken down by his own private secretary, when the question of moustaches and the proposed abolition of whiskers came before the Army Council in about the tenth year of his command.

The Duke was then in the very zenith of his powers; and any element of opposition (in the Country almost non-existent, for there had been no war since his appointment; and in the Council itself fractional) found voice in only a certain Brigadier-General who, greatly daring and alone, allowed himself occasionally to pass from respectful representation to something that sounded like criticism.

Until that date the whisker had been, *par excellence*, the adornment of the military profession; now the moustache was becoming its rival; and an attempt was even being made in certain quarters (led by the Brigadier-General) to oust it, altogether, from the regulations, and have moustaches alone.

The Duke himself stood strongly for both; to him the matter was a personal one. Having taken his whiskers into active service, he had come back like others with an added moustache. This circumstance for him made history. And it was from this standpoint that, on the occasion recorded, he took up his parable and spoke.

'In the matter which is before us for discussion,' he said, 'it is of vital importance, and two things which we have to bear in mind, that the professional soldier should by his appearance, and all that, make himself attractive to the softer sex, and at the same time not only terrific but repulsive to the enemy, – in a word irresistible to both.

'Now it is by a merciful provision of Providence that, in this respect, women are won by that which makes men appear more formidable. A ferocious moustache, and all that sort of thing, is equally a weapon of love and a weapon of war. You use them separately, but they go together. Add whiskers, of a proper shape, and they enhance the effect in either direction.

'Now if that is true about whiskers, as to my mind it certainly is, it puts the abolition of whiskers in the Army out of discussion; and the question that pre-eminently remains is – what is the proper shape of the whisker to be?

'I submit, gentlemen, that to be effective it should be large, that it should stand out, and all that sort of thing – not lying flat or cut short – and that it should begin in line with the moustache.

'In Italy, as you may know, a moustache has been invented, under Royal patronage, the King himself wearing it, which I commend very specially to your notice as instructive. It is a continuation into whisker – so shaped that you cannot tell where whisker begins and where moustache leaves off. It is called a mustachio, from the addition, I believe, of the Latin word "eo," to go – it is a moustache, that is to say, which goes on and doesn't have to stop. It certainly presents a very fine appearance at reviews and occasions of that kind, and I believe is largely responsible for the enthusiasm with which his troops greet him whenever he appears on parade. I understand also, that the effect is not confined to the troops; but that on women as well – however, into that perhaps I need not now go; it only bears out what I was saying.

'Now I myself should be decisively in favour of that form of moustache-cum-whisker, if we ourselves had first invented it; since it would meet the wishes of those who wish to do away with whiskers, and of those who, like myself, wish to retain them. But I cannot help feeling that we must not allow it to be said that we are imitating the foreigner or importing anything from abroad. In the Army we must be native in our traditions and practice. For that reason, therefore, I fear that we cannot adopt this compromise, which would otherwise be so satisfactory to both sets of opinion. For that I am very

sorry. I have mentioned it to show that I have
not overlooked it; and that I have not rejected
it without serious consideration.

'This brings us then to a position which
makes compromise difficult, or even impossible.
For, gentlemen, I say plainly – to those who
desire me to remain Commander-in-Chief of
the Army – that I am not going to give up my
whiskers. If they have to go, I retire. They
accompanied me into battle, and I brought
them safe out of battle; and if they had been
shot off I should have grown them again; and
they shall go down with me honourably into
the grave.

'If, therefore, I am to remain your chief, and
the Army's chief – and I may as well tell you
that the Queen herself has informed me that
she likes whiskers, and all that – then the only
question before us is what shape is the whisker
going to be?

'Now unfortunately – and this is the cause of
all the trouble – owing to civilians imitating the
Army, and while imitating making it different,
the whisker we wear has come to be called by
the very undignified and unmilitary name of
a "mutton-chop" whisker; and unfortunately,
gentlemen, mutton-chop suggests sheep; and
sheep are not a proper suggestion for an Army.

Therefore, it may be, that the "mutton-chop" whisker will have to go, so far as the Army is concerned.

'Just the same sort of thing happened in the Navy; there, the whisker which goes round under the chin, came to be called the "marmoset" whisker. I've no doubt it was some mischief-makers who did it; and the result was that the "marmoset" whisker has had to go.

'Therefore we have to be very careful what shape we are going to adopt; because if you wore downward whiskers large and curved and triangular, you would get some wag calling them "the wings of the dove"; and that certainly wouldn't do. Therefore we must find a shape that shall be – shall be – '

The Duke paused for a word.

'Impervious to epigram,' suggested the Brigadier-General.

'Yes, impervious, and – ' the Duke was not quite sure what impervious meant, so he added a word the meaning of which he did know; '*and* imperious.'

'Impervious and imperious,' mused the Brigadier-General. 'Epigrammatic themselves in fact?'

'Yes,' agreed the Duke, 'as epigrammatic as you can make 'em. Therefore I suggest that they should be shaped like a battle-axe, and stand out sideways to right and left, in a rich curl.'

'Rather an obsolete weapon – the battle-axe, don't you think, Sir?' commented the Brigadier-General.

The Duke scented the satire of this criticism, and made a good reply: 'So is the lion an obsolete animal throughout Europe,' he replied. 'So is the unicorn; so is the double-headed eagle; but there you have them on Royal standards, and they go into battles and win them! When we talk about shapes in the Army we are talking about symbols. Brigadier, you are always opposing me.'

'Only making suggestions, Sir,' replied the Brigadier-General suavely. 'If my suggestions appear costive, I apologize.'

'Costive?' said the Duke: 'we haven't been discussing cost: whiskers don't cost anything – they save; less work for the barber, less shaving to do. There's another reason in their favour.'

'But if they are to be curled, Sir – like a battle-axe, you said – ' queried the Brigadier-General, persistent in underhand opposition, 'does Your Highness propose that the men, whose whiskers do not curl naturally, should put them into curl-papers at night?'

The Duke was silent for a moment; he was thinking. Should he admit that, in his young days, before the fashion shortened, and when its big flowing curl was the very essence of a whisker – should he admit that he *had* worn them – had put them into curl-papers at night?

No: such a divagation into the past was unnecessary. Instead he merely remarked, '*What* they do at night, *how* they do it, so long as they are in barracks to time, matters nothing. You issue an army-order, you say whiskers are to be curled, and they *are* curled. And whether God gives it them, or the barber gives it them, or whether they give it themselves, doesn't matter to me. Army orders are all that I am concerned about.'

And there the record stops short; and we don't know what actually was decided in the matter.

What we do know is that, in fact, whiskers gradually went out of fashion, both in the army and out of it, the moustache alone taking their place. And in course of time – but that was after the Duke's death – moustaches followed and disappeared also, in favour of smooth-shavenness. And some day, no doubt, whiskers will reappear in the army, and will have a shape of their own which will be thought military; but will they ever come back – as the Duke would have liked them to do – curled, and shaped like a battle-axe?

CHAPTER XVIII

A SYMBOLIC ACT

THE instinct of inhèrited rank – the habit of
authority – enables its possessor to do, almost
unconsciously, deeds which men of meaner
prestige would never dare. This is what marks
your true aristocracy. A British Ambassador,
in the days when bicycles were an innovation,
bicycled without shame in the streets of Con-
stantinople; whereupon a Turkish Pasha made
the just commentary: 'It takes a great man to
do that.'

The Pasha was pleased that an act so independent of the conventions could be so
naturally done without loss of dignity. And it
is with a like pleasure, as we approach the end
of the Duke's career, that we record a similar
act done by him, on a most public occasion,
proving the power of initiative possessed for
emergency by one of Royal Blood.

The statue of the Duke, erected within two

253

years of his death, stands on the site of his most famous exploit, or, at least, within a hundred yards of it. And, speaking of Armies and the goose-step, what do a hundred yards matter? They are soon covered.

A hundred yards from where he now sits on his horse, – better than ever he sat on it in real life – the deed was done which proved this at least about the Army which, under the Duke's control, had so beautifully marked time; that whatever had happened to its buttons, its boots, and the manly growth which in those days compulsorily fringed its lips – it still had a Commander-in-Chief capable of going any-where in all weathers and doing anything.

But, in that statue, what a chance of sym-bolism combined with impressive composition the sculptor has missed! Perhaps his com-mission did not allow of it; perhaps a timorous Army Council ruled it out as contrary to the regulations, above which, like Nelson with his blind eye, he then set himself; perhaps the funds available might not have covered the large expenditure on bronze which a figure so canopied would have required. And yet that commemorable deed was, in truth, the un-conscious prophecy of a new age, with its vast mechanization of the Army to meet actual conditions, which till then its tradition had been obstinately to ignore: bearskins, busbies, and helmets to promote headache and fatigue; red tunics and glittering cuirasses to make better targets for the enemy; pipe-clayed trimmings carefully devised to give to every individual soldier each day as much house-maid's work of rubbing, scrubbing, powdering and polishing as was humanly possible in order to fill up their useless time, and divert them domestically from thoughts of blood; tight boots to ration the day's march; padded chests for the encouragement of weak hearts, and for the introduction – when pierced by bullets – of horsehair and cotton-wool into the system; the goose-step, with its pretty pattern and its negation of muscular freedom, but valuable in a volunteer army as a symbol of readiness to face death – a stiffening of resolve as well as of kneecaps and calves: 'Gentlemen of the some-thing or other, fire first, for we are certain to arrive last! Knock us down like ninepins; but like ninepins we shall get up again!' You cannot show fear while you keep a stiff knee; the goose-step was, therefore, a device for the automatic banishing of fear from a well-trained Army: this, and the quivering salute in the face of the King's Commission. Abolish the goose-

step, and fear would enter; forgo the salute
and respect for the machine would vanish! All
that – though we still keep it on parade – all
(except the salute) has now gone! And though
the Duke pinned his dear faith on it, and
believed that without each and every item, here
above recited, Army and Empire would crash
down to perdition, his nevertheless was the
hand which raised on that historic occasion the
standard of revolt – the revolt of on-coming
common sense, and the adaptation of the species
to its environment.

It was a wet day, Queen Augusta liked wet
days; the Duke did not, nor did the Army, nor
did the public which had to come to look on.
But this was a Trooping of the Colours in the
Queen's honour; and Heaven had com-
plimentarily sent the weather she liked best to
grace the occasion.

The Life Guards stood quadrilateral, drip-
ping with wet, making the very ground wetter
with their accumulated drippings as they stood
and waited; marched splendidly, miserable in
their sunshine array, with never a sunbeam to
show on it. A thousand pounds' damage per
hour was being done to their tunics alone. The
drums beat out of tune; the gravel of the parade-
ground became a sobbing mush; the regi-

mental colours hung like sheep's liver; and the thing was going to last for two mortal hours!

Into this situation of magnificent nonsense, the Duke, as he took up his position, let off, into the spiritual ears of posterity, a soundless bomb of common sense. Dumb then, the wonder of it reverberates still.

He took from the hand of a waiting orderly – the elastic trigger or time-fuse of the weapon having already been unhitched – an umbrella of corded silk, large, black, and impenetrable; and with an upward and forward jerk unfurled it over his cock-plumed head; and under it raised his hand solemnly to the salute.

And there, in the person of its Commander-in-Chief, the Army recognized for the first time in its existence at a Trooping of the Colours – that it did actually rain, and that rain spoils uniforms, and settles down into the hollows of saddles, giving old, old generals that squat in it chills, rheumatic pains, lumbagos, and sciaticas – leaving no choice to their victims which of them it is to be.

The Nation – the Army – did not know it at the time. But that was verily the beginning of the end; the age of scarlet-fevered militarism and open-air battle fronts was over; and the age of khaki for mud, and putties for marching and tanks for attack and trenches for retirement had begun.[1] And if only the War Office could have seen it, what a magnificent prophetic spectacle it would have made, had it been ordained that at the next trooping of the colours in wet weather, not one but five thousand umbrellas should be unfurled, making the tortoise as a military formation once more, after the lapse of two thousand years or so, live again!

Or failing that, had the Board of Works, or whatever department finally supervised the design and erection of the Duke's statue, had it but recognized that here and thus the prophetic gesture had taken place before the public eye; and in commemoration of that brave act – farseeing or instinctive, call it which you will – had it but canopied the Duke's equestrian statue with an umbrella of bronze, what a setting forth of history that monument would have become; and how American tourists would have flocked, and how, on the anniversary of the day, wreaths and floral umbrellas would have been laid, and crowds gathered to gaze.

[1] The Editor has here ventured to bring a prophetic passage up to date.

And, above all, how very characteristic of the Duke, in his curious blend of the domestic with the martial virtues, the statue would have been.

It was a lost opportunity. But though no monumental bronze records the deed, in a dark corner of the Military Museum a discerning mind has collected together in a glass case certain personal relics of the Duke; and among them – surely the very one, else why should it be there? – an umbrella of corded silk, black, with polished ferrule, gold band and handle of horn.

CHAPTER XIX

RETIREMENT

WITH hands frequently crippled from gout, the
Duke continued to fulfil the duties of his high
office, making on an average five hundred
signatures *per diem*. But though he thus
struggled to keep his own personal mark impressed on it, the Army was getting beyond
him.

It was an unfortunate circumstance that
most of the wars it had to wage were not
civilized wars. They took place under conditions which he had never had the opportunity
of studying, and too far away for his personal
supervision to be possible. And the commanders who were given the direction, would
endeavour, when the campaign was over, to
secure the application of their experience under
outlandish conditions to the Army at home.

This, of course, was resisted by the Duke as a
non-sequitur. A European war would be a very

different thing from a Colonial; and for a European war he felt that he possessed all the necessary tradition and authority. How war should be conducted in a civilized country was shown by the annual Army manœuvres over which he presided; in his view no better example could be devised.

But a new school was growing up, and had even become a majority in the Army Council (of which – though rather deaf – he was still the head), which thought differently. And more and more, with a certain Adjutant-General leading them, the majority would not give way to his opinion. And when, after long contention, the votes of the majority were referred to the Civil Ministry, the Duke's would be overruled; a thing which in the old days had never happened. Commander-in-Chief had now become a mere name. He was able to delay changes, but could not avert them.

Coming back from these Councils, he would go straight to his bed, and stay in it sometimes for two or three days, soothed by the kind presence of his wife, who came and sat beside him, and listened sympathetically to his plaint. 'I have become a cipher,' he said.

'You are getting old,' she answered. 'Why not take a holiday?' She never suggested that he should resign, though that perhaps is what she really meant.

And resignation never for a moment entered his mind: till one day – very respectfully, and with many compliments over what he had done in the past – it was asked of him by the Civil Minister of War in the Prime Minister's name. The Government had decided on the re-organization of the Army; and under the new scheme so much decentralization into different departments would take place, that the post of Commander-in-Chief could no longer stand.

The Duke sat and listened while the scheme was expounded to him; he recognized it without difficulty as the invention of the Adjutant-General, who, under its provisions, would have the practical control of it. He had heard it all before from the Adjutant-General himself, and had turned it down. And now the Adjutant-General had gone with it behind his back, and the Government had accepted it. There the whole thing was, before his eyes, complete: not a skeleton, not a rough draft, but a finished and detailed state document with all its intricacies related and fixed. It meant that, without his knowing a word of it, the revolution and destruction of his beloved Army had been planned.

OLD WOOLCESTER CHURCH (NOW DESTROYED)
WHERE THE FITZ-WILLIAM MARRIAGE TOOK
PLACE

He sat silent for a while; then he said, 'And God damn it, sir, what if I refuse to resign?'

Very respectfully he was informed that it had become a matter of policy: that the scheme would go forward and be made an Act of Parliament.

'Call it, then,' said the Duke, 'by its proper name: An Act for the dismissal of the Commander-in-Chief.'

'Oh, not at all,' he was politely answered. But he had said his last word. He got up, and he went out; and never, as Commander-in-Chief, did he enter the War Office again.

He went home and to bed; but did not send in his resignation. And he would never have done so, had not Queen Augusta herself asked him for it as a personal favour.

To that expedient the Ministry had been forced. She, ardently agreeing with the Duke, sad, outraged, indignant, did nevertheless her constitutional duty on the advice of her Ministers, and secured that preservation of appearances which the relation between Crown and Government require.

'My Army,' she wrote, 'will never be the same, with you no longer at the head of it. And some day when it is too *late*, they will learn their *mistake*. I do not think that I have ever had a Ministry so *obstinate*; but what I mind most is the *ingratitude*, and lack of consideration which they have shown to you. What *my own feelings* are in the matter, I shall presently have the opportunity of making *quite plain.*'

The Duke sent his resignation personally to the Queen; and having done so, consented that it should be re-written for communication to the Press. But though, in the published version, it mentioned age, the Duke would not allow the word 'infirmity.' He was still, in his own estimation, sufficiently sound in mind and body to continue in the position which had been his for nearly forty years.

The Queen's mind was 'made plain' by the creation of a new Order for the reward of long public service. No one, it was understood, who had served less than a quarter of a century would be eligible for it, nor anyone whose record had not secured the Sovereign's personal confidence and approval. Thus, since there was no other honour which the Duke did not already hold, he became Grand Commander of the Order of Her Majesty's Service, and *first* personal Aide-de-camp, the word 'first' being an honorific addition to an appointment which was already his.

Though the Duke's retirement from office was a great relief to everybody except himself and the Crown, the complimentary mourning over it in the Press was deep and splendid. Everything was done as handsomely as possible to give an apparent substance to the pretence that the Army had lost a great administrator, and the Nation a wise and valuable servant. And the Duke did, indeed, read these tributes of the Press with a flicker of satisfaction; they were a testimonial, the sincerity of which he did not for a moment doubt, and a justification which he felt that he had earned. But what pleased him even more was the burst of popularity with which he was greeted when, appearing on horseback for the last time, he rode in the great procession commemorative of the Sovereign's reign which took place in the following year.

Of his popularity there could be no doubt; and whether the virtue which produced it was in the main his or the public's, or a nice combination of both, it is pleasant to record that on that, his last decisive appearance in public, he was greeted enthusiastically and affectionately by a crowd three or four miles long, and the cheers of over a million people.

The Army gave him a farewell banquet; and his reception was tremendous. The speech he made on that occasion was considered the best he had ever made. And at the end of it, though there were some dry eyes there were many wet ones, including the Duke's own.

The report, from which the following extracts are taken, was probably not quite verbatim: but it gives very faithfully the style of the Duke's oratory, with those little lapses from grammar which were so characteristic and so endearing:

'MY LORDS, AND BROTHER OFFICERS,

'My feelings on this occasion, when I rise as I do, and what I am about to say, are indescribable. You will not, I am sure, Gentlemen, if any such are here, wish me to go into matters about things that one would not wish to be mentioned, – and here least, on any account. God takes the hindmost and the foremost of all of us; and the least said the soonest mended. All I do wish to say, and will say, and which it would be very painful for me to have to say otherwise, is that I have to the best of my knowledge, and belief, and experience – I only put it at that – always done my duty as I believed it to be. And while I have had a great many friends, more of them surviving than I do, but some now gone alas to their just account – men who have helped and supported me, and all that, and have some-times had to differ from them, and they from me, – I can truly say, and I do with great thankfulness, now that everything for me is over, except having to die in my bed instead of on a field of battle, that I have not con-sciously made an enemy in my own country.

'And if the Army is still made of the men it used to be made of, it will remain an Army, and, by God, a fine Army! But if it is made of men different from the men it used to be made of, then all I can say is I don't know what it will be like, or whether it will be like an Army at all.

'And having said that, not meaning it to be personal to anyone who is here, or not here, you will excuse my feeling if I only say I thank you all from the bottom of my heart for the way in which you have drunk my health. And though, at my age, one can't expect to have too much of it, I hope to have enough to go on for a few years yet. And the Army, God bless it, and keep it, and continue it, as *He* would always have it to be, and as *I* would always have it to be. Gentlemen, I thank you.'

Somebody said of him, who was present on that occasion, that he was 'an old fool, but a great gentleman.' And if that is the truth about him, there is good reason for the mingled memory and oblivion into which his name and career have now passed.

Rough tempered, and sometimes bearish, he yet managed to make himself liked by those under him; and though he carried a grievance, he bore no grudge. Even with the Adjutant-General, who had been the main cause of his retirement, he remained on polite speaking terms; and now and then would look in on him, during office hours, to inquire benevolently how things were getting on. And sometimes, to humour the old man, the Adjutant-General would make a show of consulting him, asking for his experience and advice. And the Duke would go away, pleased; and returning home, 'They miss me!' he would say to his wife. 'They miss me!'

One day, hobbling in from the street to the Staff Office, where the Adjutant-General was busily at work, and going in as usual unannounced, he stood in the door to make the usual inquiry: 'And how is my poor Army getting on?'

'O nicely, nicely!' the General answered him, 'recruiting is going well.'

The Duke dived a hand into his pocket, fetched something out of it, and presented it for inspection.

'See that?' he demanded.

The Adjutant did see. It was a button.

'Do you know where that button came from?' he was asked.

'Before it came out of your pocket? No, Sir.'

'You don't know what that button belongs to?'

The Adjutant had not the expert's eye for buttons; their origin and antecedents escaped him. He owned it. The Duke's tone was triumphant.

'That,' he said, 'is the hind button of a Life Guardsman's trousers. Just now, as I went by, they were changing guard. I heard it fall off. Buttons didn't fall off the Army in my day.'

'An exception to prove the rule,' suggested the Adjutant. But the Duke would admit no exception in the matter of buttons.

'If you have one falling off,' he said, 'you may have 'em all falling off. You can't conduct a charge of cavalry, if its buttons aren't safe. This sort of thing didn't happen in my day.'

He put the button back in his pocket, and

269

carried it off to his museum as a memento –
there to be labelled, dated and catalogued:
'Button which fell off the Army into the street,
during peace time, picked up by the Duke of
Flamborough as he was passing the War Office,
and shown by him to the Adjutant-General.'

An historic button therefore.

But what has now become of it? For with
the Duke's death, his collection of buttons was
dispersed, nobody sufficiently caring about, or
seeing the value of it.

Yet with his collection of buttons, condemned
to leisure, the Duke had comforted his broken
heart; and his last years were spent in making
a catalogue of it. And had he for a moment
doubted the recognition of its historical value,
he would surely have made a special entry in
his will bequeathing it to the Nation. But such
a doubt never entered his mind. And his
simple faith and early views remained with him
intact till the day of his death.

CHAPTER XX

FINAL YEARS

ONLY a few crumpled and withered years now remain to be told of; years in which no event took place. As age grew on him, and deafness, he developed a habit of talking to himself; for himself he could hear, or at least could know what he was saying, and could agree with it.

The only other person he could talk to with similar comfort was his wife, who also – even if she did not – always appeared to agree with him; she being one of those wise ones who know that to disagree with certain people, when their minds and observances follow the habit of years, is no use whatever. And she had a taking habit of being companionable and responsive by gesture and play of countenance which, as she sat and knitted, quite satisfied him.

To her he could safely criticize the Army, the

271

Church, the State, the Crown itself, and above all the Age, – the desolating and deteriorating Age in which they were condemned to spend their declining years. And he would watch her fingers, knitting agreement into the triangular round of her needles as she made socks and woollies for deep-sea fishermen. So might Penelope, after her own deep-sea fisherman had come back to her for good, have spent the evening of her days combining attention to her old man with domestic handicraft.

They always sat in the same pair of chairs to right and left of the fireplace. And the Duke himself would lean over, and poke, and make up the fire, when the fire required it, without ringing for it to be done. And as the old couple kept fires going late into spring, and started them again early in autumn, that fire-side habit formed, in final years, the major part of their domestic life – that, and the comfortable bed which they shared. For the new fashion, which was then springing up, of twin bedsteads placed side by side never pleased them; and the Duke to the end of his days wore nightshirts, preferring to have the renewed acquaintance of his legs, such as they were, after their enforced separation from each other during the day.

Now and then their children, who had

become middle-aged people with establishments of their own, would look in to see them; but though welcome when they came, they were not wanted. The life of the old couple, though narrow, was singularly complete.

When the Duke was at last compulsorily retired from the command of that great engine of destruction which had become so inefficient in his hands, his wife did not cry over it, or denounce, or complain. To her it had been a waiting event, of which, years before it happened, her common sense had made her expectantly aware.

But she was very nice about it, and stroked his hand – that inefficient, gouty old hand, from which the sword of military maintenance had been taken – and coaxed him to look at things which, though smaller, had a brighter side. After all, she had borne his sons, and three were in the Army and doing well at it – so she supposed – since at quite an early age they had become Colonels. They were there to carry on the tradition, to see that buttons were bright, and knees stiff at the goose-step and dressings straight, and the salute given with a quiver, as in God-fearing days had been laid down, and as it still ought to be so long as God is recognized as the God of Battles, and the Army with its discipline upreaching rank upon rank into the heights above, as His best representative on Earth.

To this order of things, which was his world, she gave an acquiescent mind; just as she would have accepted other worlds had they suited him better. For she was one who took things as they came mildly and without criticism, but having her own mind about them all the same.

It was of things like these, when his heart was broken from office, that the Duke talked to his wife or to himself, sitting cosy and warm by the fire in the late evening of his days. And for a while it was a comfortable sort of grief which had possession of him – comfortable, in so far as he had at the back of it the sense of duty done, and by his side a sympathetic ear in which to complain. And if only a kind Providence would have seen to it that his wife outlived him he would have died comfortably occupied with his grievance, and happy with his good listener.

But Providence was not kind; and during the last eighteen months of his life, he sat facing an empty chair (receiving from it only a ghost of the response he had been accustomed to) – talking to himself, talking to it, and no longer making up the fire himself, or even ringing for it to be done. Attendants, unsummoned, had to come in and out and see to things. And once, so entering, found him sunk in his chair in a posture from which he had no longer the ability to raise himself.

From his chair he was carried up to his bed – the same shared bed of old, now unnecessarily large for its single occupant – and a week later had qualified for the public funeral which then became his due.

The blinds of his official residence were decorously drawn down for the occasion; even as a week previously straw had been laid along the street-front of it to prepare the public mind. And though he was not there, bulletins were posted at the door, and callers admitted to make inquiry and to leave signatures. Across the Duke's attachment to the shadow of his hidden life, the old veil of subterfuge had still to be drawn.

A few hours after his death, at the dead of night, his coffined body was brought across from the little house in the side street which it had so comfortably occupied, through back-door, and stone-flagged garden, and was put to lie in state under the roof which had never been its home; but where it had received Shahs

275

and Emperors, and foreign Royalties, and held military levees, and given dinners at which every one wore military stars, only a few of which had been acquired to the sound of guns, or within range of rifle bullet, for these were all staff-officers or dignitaries whose base was at the War Office.

And just as, over the preliminaries of his state funeral, a smoke-screen was drawn to hide from the public view the too domestic circumstances of his death, so similarly over the spot where he lies buried.

In the Chapel Royal at Crown Castle, a recumbent figure, with waist measurements somewhat reduced, forms his memorial in stone. It wears peer's robes and orders of knighthood over a military uniform; and because cocked hats cannot adjust themselves to tombs as mediaeval helmets used to do, a cocked hat is tucked inconspicuously under the left arm. The right hand carries a marshal's baton, at the feet a small lion occupies a subsidiary position, the Duke's boots resting against its side.

But the Duke himself, in bodily remainder, is not there. He had left in his will strict injunctions that he and his wife should lie together; and she lies, according to her station, unpretentiously as she lived, in a place where royal bodies do not congregate.

Perhaps her previous demise decided the matter; for since the law – even had the Crown consented to the innovation – would have required an order of disinterment to enable her to come and lie by him, it was deemed better to arrange matters the other way; and when the state funeral was well over, in the quiet dead of night the Duke's body went out once more by a back-door, and was inconspicuously hearsed to its final resting-place. And the white marble stone which marks the spot bears record of her alone, though in the wording of it there is reference to the 'faithful and sorrowing Husband' who lies nameless at her side.

The Duke, as he passed from the scene, had a 'good Press.' All the papers spoke handsomely of him. The usual things said concerning the shortcomings of other military commanders when death brings them to book were not said of him. The voice of criticism was hushed; his career was viewed rather as a monument than as a movement in the life of the Nation – a terminal landmark indicative of an age that had passed.

EDITOR'S FOOTNOTE

THIS is a valet's life of one who could have been no man's hero; but whose birth, nevertheless, brought him hazardously near to the throne of an ancient and wise people, and gave him, for the better part of two generations, the mismanagement of its army.

And had he come to the throne, the people would have accepted him, as they accept the conventions of institutional religion, with all the outward appearances of belief. And throughout his life a smoke-screen of fine phrases would have gone up concerning him, obscuring the fact of his more than average ordinariness, for the sake of the monarchical system which he stood to adorn.

And if this is an illustration of our wonderful charity toward Kings, would it not be well that we applied it more widely? For if we can make so much of the indifferent material to which hereditary monarchy is sometimes reduced, and are willing to treat its exponents so handsomely, ignoring their deficiencies, can we not

MR. BENJAMIN BUNNY

also do better by average human nature, which is so much more with us, and in the bulk so much more important in its wide-reaching effects on the moral and intellectual progress of the race?

This is the moral which Mr. Benjamin Bunny's revaluation of the Duke of Flamborough's career seems to suggest. He may not always have been quite fair to him; personal disappointment may have embittered his estimate of the man on whose private life circumstances enabled him to spy, and into whose private papers he made an unlicensed inroad for the materials of this biography. But few unprejudiced readers can doubt that his estimate is nearer the truth than that which was supplied for public consumption during the Duke's life, or immediately after his death. And if so much credit could, with generous pretence, be given where so little was due, what an enormous difference it would make to the world could it in like measure, be given to all! How rose-coloured human nature would then appear; or rather, not human nature so much as human achievement.

For in these pages Mr. Bunny makes the Duke to appear more likeable – more lovable even – than anything in the official 'Life'

suggests. Yet by many, the bleak colourlessness
of that official cenotaph, so whitened and so
empty, will be greatly preferred, for the
decorous oblivion which it ponderously
bestows.

Mr. Bunny's offence – if offence it be –
against a surviving taste for dishonesty where
the memorials of Royalty are concerned, is
that, while the official 'Life' does so without
knowing it, he knowingly exposes the ridiculous
side of the Duke's standing in history. In the
one it can be politely ignored; in the other it
cannot. And the book he has written brings
out the real ridiculousness into which Royalty
betrayed a worthy but inefficient character.
The education which Royalty imposed on him
was rather more ridiculous than the average
education – bad though it was – of that day;
and the results on his life and character were
ridiculous in proportion, adding ridiculous
opinions and ridiculous habits to a mind
which had already a natural bent in that
direction.

It was ridiculous to make a man of poor
average capacity the head of the military
machine which the prejudices and policies of
the age still found supremely important to the
life of the Nation. It was ridiculous to make a

man of poor mental and linguistic ability, and strong foreign accent, stand up and deliver speeches on all sorts of subjects about which he had neither knowledge, nor thought, nor interest. And it was ridiculous when he died to set up a large and imposing statue to such a man in a commanding position in the metropolis of a great nation. It was incidentally ridiculous to put him on horseback at all – whether in statue or in life; he always disliked it, and did ill at it. But since, in a statue, a horse serves to keep up appearances, there he sits horsed, dividing the traffic and a little obstructing it – even as the statue of Royalty is now dividing and slightly obstructing the forward movement of men's minds, and the mobility of their institutions.

But in all this olla-podrida of foolishness, to which a poor simple humdrum character was held down by a dynastic fate – this forced adaptation of a nature, natively shy, to a life of public parade, there stood to his credit the one sensible thing that he had done on his own initiative without consulting anyone – his private and morganatic marriage.

It was not merely sensible, it was a success – was curative, remedial, corrective, having healing in its wings. It gave to him moments, hours, regular hours, every day and every night, during which he could resume normality of thought, feeling, affection, and become a natural character again – himself and nothing else: an irascible but fond father, a faithful and respectful husband, recognizing the superiority of his wife's character and mental equipment; a fire-side person who liked to get into slippers, have a glass of toddy at his side, and read the Conservative newspapers and periodicals in a place where the public could not get at him, not even knowing his address.

And this one sensible thing was pushed out of sight, made invisible, officially ignored, the public not being supposed to know of it. Only very distantly and reticently does the official 'Life' say anything about that – the so much better part of him – which gave genuine human colour to his existence.

The rest of his life is the price he paid to Royalty – the price it demanded of him; that he should be something all his days, away from his own nature, consistently contrary to common sense. And without a glimmer of a notion that it meant a double wastefulness, he gave to his own order the service that it required of him, believing heart and soul that the institution of Monarchy was the most useful of all devices to keep the world and religion and politics from going to the dogs.

And though to some its tendency may seem different and contrary, no one can deny that a use is still found for it; and many of its users will desperately cling to it, when the time comes for its removal, and perhaps even fight for it as the living symbol of all the atavisms of a system they still wish to preserve. And having so set their faith on it, and made it a part of their religion, they object to having it criticized. You may not even criticize it for the values it has lost under the commercial twist which vested interests have given it. Royalty, having been reduced to a safe average of ordinariness, is to stand representatively sacred, on a spot that has been well fenced in; and the last thing it must ever do is to shock or startle the public conscience by a symbolic act of unexpected representativeness to which men's minds might unconventionally respond. We have a commercial, but we have no longer a courageous use for Royalty.

Yet the courage is sometimes there waiting to be used; and perhaps the best things done by Royalty in recent years have been things very unofficial and unrecorded.

And since I have thus ventured to criticize the impoverished use which the well-to-do mind of the Nation now makes of Royalty, I will give an instance the other way, of which perhaps very few will have heard.

To a hospital, on an official visit, goes a young Prince, charming, popular, with a gift for doing unconventional things which are sometimes a little embarrassing to the official mind. The hospital to be visited on this occasion, was a hospital in which some hundreds of the most helpless and unpresentable victims of the War are to this day kept out of public sight, for fear lest we should realize in all its ghastliness what war means.

Into this receptacle of shelved humanity goes the young Prince. Officially received, officially conducted from ward to ward, he sees and speaks to some scores of the men by whose stripes in war the nation is supposed to have been healed. And having completed the official survey, he happens unconventionally to ask, 'Have I seen all?'

No; it is admitted by the officials that he has not been taken into a ward where the less presentable cases are congregated – cases too dreadful to look at and keep a good appetite afterwards. Contrary to official calculation no doubt, Royalty says: 'I must see them.' And does.

And that ordeal over, he asks again, 'Have I now seen all?'

Yes, really all this time, all except one: a case that nobody sees—a case unimaginably horrible to look at. And once more, contrary to official calculation, Royalty unexpectedly persists and does the courageous thing.

He goes in, and sees an object without eyes, without face; how much more of the body blown away – how little else left for life and the communications of life one does not know; whether able to be told, so as to understand, that the heir to the Crown had come to visit him, one does not know. Helpless before that spectacle of unhappy survival, helpless to do anything but to perform an act of human sympathy, the young Prince bent and kissed – what was left; and from that Presence went out white and shaken, but having done for the Nation the unexpectedly representative and the most truly royal thing which under the circumstances could be done.

One feels, perhaps, that it has more value told of years after it happened, than had it received the usual advertisement of the daily

Press which does so much to vulgarize alike the small and the large courtesies of Royalty.

But there are times when great and immediate publicity is the essential accompaniment to an act royally conceived and performed; and times when the Nation greatly needs to have such an act done for it. Many years ago a King owned himself responsible for the murder of one of his subjects – a rather obstreperous and resisting one – did public penance for it, and was not less kingly in so doing. The act stands out in history.

In recent years a bloody and blundering crime was done by the agents of this country, at a place called Amritsar. The Government denounced the act, and dismissed the perpetrator of it; the Country was ashamed of it; but nothing was done, sufficiently expressive of the Nation's sorrow and shame, to touch and convince the heart of the Indian people. Shortly after, we sent out the Prince of Wales as our representative to India. The ill done at Amritsar made the success of that official visit impossible; native feeling was expressed in a boycott which followed the Prince wherever he went.

It was then in our power to make Royalty the symbol of our conscience, for the reparation

286

of a great wrong; but we had not the courage or the imagination to do it. But had the Prince, on his first coming, stood, as our representative, bare-headed on the site of the Amritsar massacre in a two minutes' silence, we should have found means once more to make a worthy and a courageous use of Royalty. It would have been an act of unendurable humiliation to certain people whom it would have been very good policy to humiliate; and – it would have won India.

And in the comparison of that two minutes' silence (which as an unexpected, unconventional and courageous act of Royalty would have been so worth doing) with that other two minutes' silence, the annual performance of which has now become a military pageant, meaning so very little – so almost nothing – as registering the Nation's will that war shall never be again – in that comparison of what Royalty is and is not used for in the public life of to-day, I find my concluding commentary on the much lighter material which I have here edited, and which would not have been worth editing had it not given some point to an uncomfortable truth.